Dedalus European Classics
General Editor: Timothy Lane

THE QUEEN OF DARKNESS

GRAZIA DELEDDA

THE QUEEN OF DARKNESS
(AND OTHER STORIES)

translated and with an introduction
by
Graham Anderson

Dedalus

Supported using public funding by

**ARTS COUNCIL
ENGLAND**

Published in the UK by Dedalus Limited
24-26, St Judith's Lane, Sawtry, Cambs, PE28 5XE
info@dedalusbooks.com
www.dedalusbooks.com

ISBN printed book 978 1 915568 15 1
ISBN ebook 978 1 915568 21 2

Dedalus is distributed in the USA & Canada by SCB Distributors
15608 South New Century Drive, Gardena, CA 90248
info@scbdistributors.com www.scbdistributors.com

Dedalus is distributed in Australia by Peribo Pty Ltd
58, Beaumont Road, Mount Kuring-gai, N.S.W. 2080
info@peribo.com.au www.peribo.com.au

First published in Italy in 1902
First published by Dedalus in 2023
Translation copyright © Graham Anderson 2023

The right of Graham Anderson to be identified as the editor & translator
of this work has been asserted by him in accordance with the Copyright,
Designs and Patents Act, 1988.

Printed & bound in the UK by Clays Elcograf S.p A.
Typeset by Marie Lane

A C.I.P. listing for this book is available on request.

THE AUTHOR

GRAZIA DELEDDA

Grazia Deledda was born in 1871 in Nuoro, Sardinia. The street where she was born has been renamed after her, via Grazia Deledda. She finished her formal education at age eleven. She published her first short story when she was sixteen and her first novel, *Stella D'Oriente* in 1890 in a Sardinian newspaper when she was nineteen. She left Nuoro for the first time in 1899 and settled in Cagliari, the principal city of Sardinia where she met the civil servant Palmiro Madesani whom she married in 1900. They then moved to Rome.

Grazia Deledda wrote her best work between 1903-1920 and established an international reputation as a novelist. Nearly all of her work in this period was set in Sardinia. She published *Elias Portolu* in 1903, *La Madre* in 1920 and won the Nobel Prize for Literature in 1926. She died in 1936 and was buried in the church of Madonna della Solitudine in Nuoro, near to where she was born.

THE TRANSLATOR

GRAHAM ANDERSON

Graham Anderson was born in London. After reading French and Italian at Cambridge, he worked on the book pages of *City Limits* and reviewed fiction for *The Independent* and *The Sunday Telegraph*. As a translator, he has developed versions of French plays, both classic and contemporary, for the NT and the Gate Theatre, with performances both here and in the USA. Publications include *The Figaro Plays* by Beaumarchais and *A Flea in her Ear* by Feydeau.

His translations for Dedalus include *Sappho* by Alphonse Daudet, *Chasing the Dream* and *A Woman's Affair* by Liane de Pougy, *This was the Man (Lui)* by Louise Colet and *This Woman, This Man (Elle et Lui)* by George Sand. He has also translated Grazia Deledda's short story collections *The Queen of Darkness* and *The Christmas Present*. He is currently translating *Marianna Sirca* by Grazia Deledda for Dedalus.

His own short fiction has won or been shortlisted for three literary prizes. He is married and lives in Oxfordshire.

CONTENTS

INTRODUCTION

The Sardinian town of Nuoro, where Grazia Deledda was born in September 1871, sits among the rugged mountains and steep valleys in the north-east of the island. If Sardinia itself had a fairly remote connection with *il continente* — mainland Italy — then this small town and its surrounding villages were another world altogether. Traditional costumes were worn, ancient customs observed and life for the agricultural majority was far from easy. The long-standing freedom to graze animals and collect firewood from uncultivated lands ended in the early nineteenth century when an edict from the Turin government, *l'Edetto della Chiusura*, allowed landowners to put up walls and fences; and Sardinian authorities began to sell off sheep pastures and cork woods to the highest bidders. Grazia Deledda was therefore fortunate to be born into one of the more well-to-do Nuorese families: her father, trained as a lawyer, had numerous business interests and owned several parcels of farming land. The fifth of seven children, his daughter grew up in relative comfort in a large three-storey house — now the Grazia Deledda Museum — built by the kindly, energetic and poetry-loving Giovanni Antonio Deledda. Grazia's mother, Francesca Cambosu, was of simpler stock, although her family, too, was not without means. Francesca spoke Sard, the island language, and could neither read nor write Italian. She was, in Grazia's eyes, a rather distant and severe woman, deeply religious, devoting her life to the upkeep of her household and the proper instruction of her children.

Deledda enjoyed only a scant formal education. At that time and in that place, a girl could only expect four years of elementary schooling, after which her destiny was to practise the domestic arts at home until the family found her a suitable husband.

A dreamy pupil, Grazia nevertheless seized on the opportunities to broaden her understanding of the world. She even returned to school for an extra year. Books became the source not simply for learning but for adventures of the imagination. By her teenage years she was writing stories and poems of her own and spending her free hours reading voraciously from the library of her uncle, a priest, and from a trunk of books left behind by a tutor in Italian whom her father had briefly employed for the benefit of his eager daughter. Some of these early efforts were published in local Sardinian papers and journals and little by little the self-taught writer began to expand her horizons. Her wide reading took her from the romantic fiction in women's magazines to the romantically-flavoured novels of Alexandre Dumas, Victor Hugo and Eugène Sue, to Manzoni's *I Promessi Sposi* and

Tolstoy's *Anna Karenina*.

While these were unusual interests for a young girl brought up in a narrow and traditional society, she still took delight, and a full part, in the many feast days and festivities which marked the calendar of her fellow *Nuoresi*. She loved the island tales and legends, the local gossip, the characters that peopled her immediate world. The urge to write about them, to describe them in her own terms, was matched by a fierce ambition. She boldly wrote to editors in Cagliari, and even in Rome, seeking an outlet for her writings. An early story, *Sangue sardo* (*Sardinian Blood*) was published in *L'ultima moda*, a Rome-based magazine, in 1888. In 1890, a short romantic novel, *Stella d'Oriente*, was serialised in a Cagliari periodical and later published in book form. Her tales of Sardinian life incurred the incomprehension and wrath of many of her connections in Nuoro, where it was unheard-of for a young woman to write in the first place, while to take themselves as subjects for her fictions was little short of shameful.

It was the serious and thoughtful reception of her novel *La via del male* (*The Way of Evil*) by the distinguished writer and literary critic Luigi Capuana in 1896 that brought Deledda to the point where she could consider her talent and ambition validated. The obstacles in her path, largely a matter of her Sardinian background (geographical and literary remoteness, social disapproval, the need to master Italian as a second language), could all be overcome.

By 1900, at which time the population of Nuoro stood at a mere 7,000, Deledda yearned for a wider life. She needed to be in Rome. She needed, also, at the age of twenty-eight, a husband. On a visit to Cagliari in 1899 Deledda was introduced to a civil servant, a secretary in the finance department named Palmiro Madesani, a good-looking and good-humoured man a few years her senior. The two were married in January 1900 and Grazia immediately pressed all her contacts, by now quite wide, to help secure her husband's transfer to Rome. And indeed, within two months Madesani had been offered a minor post in the Finance Ministry there. By the middle of March, the couple was installed in an apartment not far from Via Nazionale, the broad avenue leading into the Piazza della Repubblica. Grazia Deledda had finally arrived.

Over the next thirty-odd years, Deledda published nearly fifty works. Most of them were novels, most of them set in Sardinia. But she also wrote upward of 250 short stories, usually collected in brief volumes (of which the present is an example), and a small number of plays. The stories ranged from Sardinian folk tales to stories for children, scenes from her own life as a girl in Nuoro, alongside the numerous brief fictions drawing on her intimate knowledge of the island of her birth.

The impressive body of her work, its distinctive, not to say unique evocations of an almost forgotten location and culture, earned her, in 1926, the Nobel Prize in Literature, which she collected at a ceremony in Sweden the following year. She was in famous company: George Bernard Shaw had won the prize for 1925, Henri Bergson was to win it for 1927. She was, however, only the second woman, after Selma Lagerlöf in 1909, to be so honoured.

It was at about the same time that health issues, which had been troubling her for some years, came to the fore. She was diagnosed with breast cancer, underwent a successful operation, but became increasingly withdrawn. She spent her final years quietly, though as industriously as ever, watching closely over the fortunes of her two sons and delighting in the company of her niece Mirella, a charming snapshot of whom appears in her 1930 collection, *Il dono di natale* (*The Christmas Present*). Sadly, the cancer returned, and Grazia Deledda died in August 1936, a few weeks before her 65th birthday.

Although her early life on Sardinia formed the bedrock of her writing career, it was the freedom of her new-found status and location that enabled her to make full use of it. To begin with, she had the much-anticipated pleasure of being able, with Madesina, to attend the opera and theatre and immerse herself in the cultural life of the capital city. Her first child, a son, Sardus, was born in December 1900; her second, Francesco, in 1904. She published a new work almost every year, earning increasingly widespread admiration and acceptance. And it was at the time of her marriage and move to Rome that she secured her first major success, the novel *Elias Portolu*, which was followed soon afterwards by this present collection of short stories, *La regina delle tenebre*. *Elias Portolu* is the story of a young man who returns to Sardinia after serving a prison sentence on the mainland. He falls in love with Maddalena, the fiancée of his brother. Unable to take the decisive step of winning her for himself, he adopts the alternative and seemingly negative course of becoming a priest. When the brother and fiancée die, and although Elias's sense of conscience had been appeased, there is a prevailing sense of cold comfort which was to be typical of many of Deledda's later works. The novel first appeared in *Nuova Antologia* in 1900, but reached wider renown when it was published in translation in the distinguished French journal *La revue des deux mondes* in 1903.

In the meantime, following a summer visit to Sardinia where, next to the church on the side of Mount Ortobene the Deledda family had a *cumbissia* (see *The Black Mare*), the short story collection *The Queen of Darkness* was published in 1902. It reveals, in compact form, the many different sides of Deledda's character as a writer. Criminality and deceit are frequent themes, as in the long story *The Black Mare*; deceit and injustice in *Two Sides of Justice* and *Sarra*; while a simpler and happier love story, *The First Kisses*, concludes the collection. The first two stories have nothing to do with peasant life on Sardinia, however. The title piece presents the journey of a mysteriously troubled soul towards the realisation that her true destiny, her salvation, is to be an artist, a writer whose purpose is to evoke and bring to life the world that has formed her. In its direction, if not necessarily in its material facts, the story has autobiographical implications. *The Lost Child* deals with another troubled soul, a lonely man driven towards suicide by unspecified causes who finds a reason for living after a night-time encounter with an unhappy small boy. These two miniature psychological dramas, played out in the minds of two middle-class protagonists, are quite different from the 'Sardinian novels' which were to become Deledda's staple fare and make her name. The sense of brooding and sadness, though, and the intense descriptions of the effects of nature, are very much part of the Deledda oeuvre. As she finds her mature voice and makes her first significant impact on the reading public, these stories stand alongside *Elias Portolu* as an important indication of what was to come.

Deledda's attitude towards her literary career was energetic and ambitious. Her inner convictions drove her to seek success and recognition, yet she was humble enough to accept criticism and advice if it came from people she respected. Her character was generally shy and retiring — even wary and suspicious, and she did not like fuss. Yet in familiar company she could be an outgoing and amusing woman. The novels and stories she wrote in her later years increasingly revealed this more relaxed and optimistic side.

Notable works over the next few years included *Cenere* (*Ashes*, 1904), *L'edera* (*The Ivy*, 1908), *Canne al vento* (*Reeds in the Wind*, 1913), *Marianna Sirca* (1915) and *La madre* (*The Mother*, 1920). After her Nobel Prize, her range widened still further. In 1930 alone, for example, she published *Il dono di natale* (*The Christmas Present*), a collection of often charming stories, sketches from her own girlhood and Sardinian fables, the novel *La casa del poeta* (*The House of the Poet*) and *Eugenia Grandet*, a translation of Balzac's 1833 novel about the repressed daughter of a miser, *Eugénie Grandet*.

After Deledda's death, a complete but unpublished novel came to light amongst her papers. It was published posthumously in 1937, and is an almost entirely autobiographical account of her earlier years in Sardinia. Its title, *Cosima*, was one of her own middle names. It describes the joys and miseries of her journey from obscurity to the threshold of an extraordinarily productive career, that of an ambitious woman in a still essentially male world.

If her name is not well known to English speakers, it is to be hoped that the coming centenary of her Nobel success and the increasing availability of her works in English will bring her once again the admiration she received in her lifetime.

Interested readers might wish to read Martha King's biography, *Grazia Deledda: A Legendary Life*, to which I am indebted for some details in the first part of this introduction. Martha King has also translated a number of Deledda's works, including *Canne al vento* and *Cosima*. *La madre*, regarded by some as Deledda's best novel, was published by Dedalus Books in M G Steegman's translation in 1987 and re-issued in 2021. And alongside *The Queen of Darkness* (*La regina delle tenebre*), Dedalus will shortly be publishing *The Christmas Present* (*Il dono di natale*) and *Marianna Sirca*.

THE QUEEN OF DARKNESS

She was beautiful, rich, engaged to be married. She had never experienced real misfortune of any kind. Then one day, at the age of twenty-five, Maria Magda quite suddenly felt in her heart an empty blackness.

It was like the onset of a physical illness, which worsened every day, growing, spreading.

She was happy in her own house, and another happiness awaited her. But in order to seize the new happiness she must abandon the old, and it seemed to her that the sorrow of leaving her family so far behind, of leaving the comforting paternal home, of losing her freedom, of abandoning the land of her birth, would be bound to inspire in her such nostalgic regret that it would poison her new happiness. There were times, especially at night, in the dark, when the prospective future filled her with deep anguish. Then she would open her eyes, stare into the dense shadows of the bedroom and think: 'No, I refuse to leave anything behind, I will not give up anything, never, never!'

And what then? The long-cherished dream of love? Ah, her happiness now, it was incomplete, it was not even happiness in comparison with the other. And at times, especially the soft, violet-shaded hours of evening, she pined as never before with desire for her distant beloved.

Sometimes she thought the true happiness might lie in merging the present and the future into one, by living with her husband in the family home.

But these moments were as lightning flashes, followed by pitch darkness. Yes, all right, and then? And then she felt that sooner or later, two, three, ten months, love would die (perhaps it was in its death agonies already if, not even married yet, she was able so clearly to envisage its end). From the grand dream all that would emerge would be a man and a woman bound together by the laws of men and not by those of the heart. But this too might not happen: yes, they would remain in love for ever, as in those novels of romance. They would have been happy all their lives, yes, fine, and then? And then it must all fall apart, time was passing, death was on its way. Ah, this was it, Magda's ailment. Or at least, in certain moments of introspection, this was what it appeared to her to be.

She could feel time passing, she could sense the vanity of all things, and deep down she had a dreadful fear of death. This fear, for a woman who still believed she could dominate events by a minute attention to the inexorable passing of time, was poisoning her life: a life to which she was so tenaciously attached. It was the idea of the coming end that arrested all impetus in its tracks, froze all joy in her heart, dried up every idea of pleasure. So, at least, she believed.

She began to become silent, withdrawn. If she went out into company, if society's entertainments made her forget her troubles, she returned home feeling hollow and disgusted with herself. Well, the entertainment was over now: why had she been so mindlessly distracted, forgetting that time was passing?

And if, instinctively, she played the scene over in her mind and, doing so, felt once more the satisfaction of her triumphs, her elegance, her splendour, an inner demon would grin derisively and mock her. Then she would draw back in disgust, amazed at how she could have lost herself in the trivialities of female vanity.

She began to remain in the house, not even going out for the ritual promenade at the approach of evening. Her only excursions were to the countryside, where she plunged into a vision of nature as if it were some holy, sweet-smelling pool, a kind of sacred immersion, driven by some powerful intuition. But even then she did not feel at peace. Even out there, surrounded by nature, the idea still pursued her of time fleeing, of the vanity of all things.

The person on whom Magda's moral sickness fell most cruelly was the distant fiancé. She did not write to him any more, or wrote him harsh letters, heaping unlikely reproaches on his head. She found him coarse and vulgar, and often, in her anger at the miseries of the world and the perfidy of society, she directed all her bitterness at him. Then she would repent, but it was a feeble and fleeting repentance. Finally, one day, analysing herself thoroughly, she believed she had found the cause of the empty darkness surrounding her. It seemed to her that she no longer loved her fiancé. And during one of her wakeful nights, she broke off the engagement, destroying a dream which had stretched long into her imagined future and which she had cherished for many long years. Everyone said she was mad, and indeed, beneath the arched line of her black and frowning eyebrows, her still blacker eyes had a fearsome gleam of folly.

At times, she even believed herself mad, and began to despair of everything. It was in this period that her behaviour became truly abnormal. She no longer left her rooms by day: she sortied out at night, taking her carriage to roam through the sleeping countryside. She wore black clothes, and over her dark hair placed a band of steel studded with five diamonds whose brilliance outshone the stars.

They began to call her then the queen of darkness. The peasants watching over their vineyards from the heights, a few shepherds sleepily following their grazing flocks in the night, a few nocturnal hunters crouching in the chilly grasses of the verges saw her more than once step down from the carriage, with those five stars of hers framing her brow, and lean against a roadside post at the lip of a sweet-smelling valley, or over the parapet of the bridge, as if transfixed by the fires on the mountainside or the hushed voice of the running water. Once, at a gathering of fashionable but uncomprehending people, a group of foolish young men fell to discussing the apparent madness of the queen of darkness. And one of them maintained, and convinced his friends, that Magda was trying to imitate Marina di Malombra* and that, like her, she would eventually commit some terrible crime. The gossip was of nothing else. Often, even Magda returned to the appalling notion that she might be losing her sanity. She sometimes felt the need to resume the old way of life, to go back into society. But more than anything else, she was held back by fear of all the talk about her strange behaviour, by the foolish curiosity her return would arouse.

And she felt sad, mortally sad; and she sought repose in the thought of death. But when, vividly, she pictured the ending of her life, the total cessation of her thoughts, her motionless corpse, the destruction of her whole proud identity, she was assailed by indescribable terror.

Eventually, one night, she went out, as usual, and stopped at the parapet overlooking the valley. She felt sadder than ever, but something unexpected, a subtle veil of tender feeling, a vague nostalgia for her distant memories, shimmered above the sadness.

Summer was coming to an end; the stars shone with brilliant purity in a moonless night sky. A new and delicate freshness hovered in the air, and the wild scents of nature rose from the valley, suffused with that faint freshness. On the distant mountains which closed off the great valley, the fires lit by the farm labourers to burn off the stubble blazed with such leaping blood-red flames that their light carried like moonlight all the way to where Magda stood. She stood there for a long time, leaning on the parapet of the bridge. In the reflections from the fires, the five diamonds sparkled like beads of dew. The water slid shallowly beneath the bridge, with a whispering murmur at once faint and continuous, thin and melancholic. On this night, even the water's voice had an unaccustomed tone, tender, like a weary voice, like a voice speaking in a dream. And the distant mountains glowed, illuminating the pure and starry darkness. There was something sublime in the spectacle, and in her intense contemplation of that mysterious darkness, Magda forgot herself, felt her sadness fall away.

The fires of those lowly workers far away seemed to cast their light on the shadows that oppressed her jewelled forehead. A deeply buried idea, perhaps existing always in the unknown depths of the psyche, shone out and suddenly revealed itself to her shadowed mind.

It came to her, the queen of darkness, that she was an artist. She felt that her restless soul contained a formidable power: to be the limpid refection of nature and of human affairs. And she thought: 'Tomorrow I shall begin to work, and my work will be like the work of those labourers who set the mountains ablaze, lighting up the night and fertilising the land. I shall describe this night, then I shall write the story of my soul. I shall return to the world, to life, to love. And the world, life and love, and my own being, will live in my works. And nothing will have the power to destroy us again.'

* *Malombra* (1881), a gothic novel by Antonio Fogazzaro (1842-1911), whose heroine, Marina di Malombra, a proud woman assailed by dark demons, murders her lover.

THE LOST BOY

A certain gentleman, Matteo Morys, had decided to commit suicide in a small wood just outside the city.

He made his will. All his household belongings he left to his elderly serving woman, and the rest of his estate to a hospital. Then one evening he made his way to the spot he had chosen for his death. He followed a route which took him through the least populated streets and soon the city was behind him. It was a fine autumn evening. The moon in its first quarter shone high in the purest of skies, and in front of Matteo, where the horizon of trees drew a black line against the sky's paler edges, a brilliant Venus was setting. The air was warm, and from far off vague noises were borne across the clear and empty spaces. It might have been springtime, and as in the lovely dusks of early May, a mysterious kind of happiness shimmered all round.

This sweet sense of life was all too evident to Matteo. And because he knew full well the enormity of what he was on his way to accomplish, there descended on him a vast grief at being no longer able to find any pleasure in living. He sensed he was dying before his time. And this was an ultimate torture, seemingly sent by destiny as the culmination of the great griefs he had already endured; and to bring it to an end as soon as possible, he quickened his pace.

He walked alone in that purest of evenings, leaving the city behind him. His shadow went before him, as if to lead him on his fatal way.

When he entered the wood, Venus was sinking like a pearl behind a little branch whose shapely leaves made perfect stencils against the sky. Matteo saw, and could not suppress a moment of anguish. From his earliest youth, a time of happy dreams, he had always loved watching the setting of Venus, even more than the setting of the sun or moon.

And this final lowering over the tree tops, more than anything else on that fatal evening, instantly reawakened in him all the dearest memories of his life. He entered the wood, following a straight and narrow avenue illuminated from on high by the moon. Not a leaf stirred: branches rose and spread, rigid, motionless in the transparent purity of the air, as if asleep in a dream of utmost peace. The moon's rays shone through them, silently making broad pools of silver on the gossamer grasses growing beneath the plants. From the ground came a chilly scent of grass, of fungus, of fallen leaves, bringing a distinct sensation of solitary and shadowy places. But even here, beneath the ever purer sky, beneath the ever clearer stars, the atmosphere was spring-like. Matteo followed the avenue and made his way directly towards a stone bench. He had often come and sat there before. It was a place where he had felt calm and serene; it was the place where he wished to die. But when he reached the end of the avenue he saw a child on the bench, fast asleep.

'At this time of night? What's going on?'

He crept carefully closer and bent over to see better. The boy, who was about four, was sitting slumped, little legs dangling, in charming abandon. His hands lay loosely on the bench, his head lolled on his chest. He was a very beautiful child, dark-haired and well dressed. He had white pumps, short black socks, embroidered shorts and a dark blue smock. The moonlight falling on him lent a faint gleam to his smooth black hair and a marble pallor to his chubby hands and small fingers. Matteo studied him for some time, holding his breath so as not to wake him. And even while he felt irritated by the pretty obstacle which had unexpectedly arisen between himself and his death, contemplating the child filled him with a kind of aesthetic but genuine tenderness.

Matteo cocked an ear, listened, stared intently all round, into the hushed depth of the moonlit avenues and glades. Complete silence. Nothing. Nobody. What should he do? Go to another part of the wood and die just the same, notwithstanding the presence of the child? No, it was not humanly possible. The sound of the shot would wake the innocent creature, terrify him. And he might be the first to discover the still warm body of the suicide. It was simply cruel. And then a curiosity to know why the boy was here, and the instinct to protect his innocent slumbers, had taken hold in Matteo's mind. And in any case, whether he died an hour sooner or an hour later, or even the next day, what did it matter?

It was clearly worth prolonging his agony in order to perform a charitable act by keeping watch over the sleeping infant. He sat down lightly on the edge of the bench, under the shadow cast by a branch, and waited, still straining his ears for the slightest sound and keeping an eye on the child. His little hands particularly held his attention. They must have been extremely cold, those little hands with their short tapering fingers. Matteo felt a strong desire to touch them, to press them in the palm of his own right hand. But fear of waking the little boy restrained him. Meanwhile time was passing, no one appeared, and the air was growing cold. That strange period of waiting, the worry and the curiosity, combined with his own sad thoughts, soon made Matteo weary. He decided to wake the child, to question him, and if possible take him back to wherever his family lived. He put out a hand, withdrew it, thought with bitterness: 'After all, what is it to me? Why get involved in an affair that could merely make trouble for me? There's nothing that ties me to life or the living any more. Let's go to another part of the wood: even if the child finds me, what does it matter? I'm no longer going to be aware of anything, after all.'

He passed a hand over his face.

'Charity? Duty?' he told himself harshly. 'I've nothing to do with life any more, and getting mixed up in this business can only extend the pain. Now that, after so many struggles, my mind is made up...'

But examining his motives more closely he realised he was interested in the sleeping child not out of charity or duty but because it gave him pleasure, a sad and sorrowful pleasure, yes, but an entirely selfish one.

A feeling for life spoke to him still. His thoughts ran on: 'But then, if it's merely a matter of my pleasure, why bother? I might as well go. Duty or pleasure, neither of them is enough to keep me in this life.'

And he stood up abruptly, regretting having allowed himself to succumb to the romantic notion of coming to die in this little wood.

'If I'd stayed at home everything would be over by now...'

He remained standing for a moment, still staring at the child. 'All right, yes, let's wake him up. And whatever happens, happens,' he thought, unexpectedly. And sitting down again next to the boy, he shook him gently. The little figure twitched, raised its head and opened two wide and frightened dark eyes, which it rapidly focussed on Matteo. The boy neither called out nor wept.

Matteo felt strangely embarrassed and could find no words to soften the boy's mute terror. It was the boy who spoke first, stammering and trying to free himself from the arm Matteo had put round him. He struggled to get down from the bench and run off.

'Let go of me... let me go...'

'Don't be frightened, little man,' Matteo said, holding him back. 'I want to help you. Listen. Don't run away, little fellow. I saw you sleeping here, all alone, at night, and since there are bad animals in these woods I had to wake you up.'

'Bad animals? Where?' the child asked, shrinking inside his clothes and shivering a little with cold as well.

'Where? They're all round, in their hiding places, and in a while they'll come out.'

'What sort of animals?'

'They're… they're all sorts, like lizards and snakes…'

'Snakes!' the boy exclaimed, now fully awake and taking everything in. 'But we have a snake. It's green, you know, and this long, look…' He held his little palms about three hand-spans apart. 'And it catches mice, you know, and it eats them.'

Matteo took hold of his hands, cold and soft, and asked him in a cajoling voice: 'Well… and what about you? Why were you sleeping here?'

The child did not answer.

'Tell me, why, little man? What's your name?'

'It's… no, I don't want to tell you, no, no…' the child said mistrustfully. He wriggled and tried to get away again. 'Let go of me, let me go.'

'But where do you want to go at this time of night? Don't you want to go home?'

'I don't want to go home.'

'I understand,' Matteo thought. 'This child has run away from home. Why?'

'Because,' he said aloud, 'you have run away from home, my fine fellow? Well, tell me. I won't take you back there, no, I'll go with you wherever you want. Where do you want me to take you?'

'No, I want to go on my own.'

'Well, at least tell me where you want to go and I'll show you the right road.'

'I don't want to tell you.'

This was getting serious. Every inquiry made the boy shake his head with distrust and try to escape from Matteo's arms.

'All right,' the latter said, getting to his feet and standing the boy upright on the bench, 'if you won't tell me, I won't let you go.'

'Then I'll bite you.'

'Ah, you little villain, you must have committed some dreadful crime. I'll have you put in prison.'

The child trembled all over and began to weep with terror.

Matteo felt remorseful. He felt his tactic had not been a good one. But he couldn't help it, he could not recall that he had ever put his arm round a child, or indeed had anything to do with one, and he did not know how to put this false step right. In fact, he made it worse.

'Listen, the night-patrol!' he said, lowering his voice, to make the child be quiet. The child had heard the word patrol before, at home, and had formed a terrifying image of it in his mind. He fell silent and clung to Matteo's chest in dread.

Then Matteo took him in his arms and made off along the narrow moonlit avenue.

'Don't be afraid,' he said in a voice that was now softer, almost moved. 'There's no need to be afraid when you're with me. I'll carry you to wherever you want to go. But tell me your name first and why you've run away from home.'

The child obstinately refused to speak.

'You see, little fellow, it's night-time now, and at night-time we can't go travelling about. We'll set off tomorrow morning. First of all, I'll take you to my house, I'll give you lots of beautiful books with pictures in them.'

'Coloured pictures?'

'Yes, coloured ones as well, you know. And on the way, you can tell me what they call you.'

'Gino.'

'Oh, well done! Gino, then…' But the child seemed to regret his admission.

'No, I'm not called Gino, I'm called something else.'

'Never mind, even if you do have a different name, I'd like to call you Gino. So, I was saying: books with beautiful coloured pictures. And then we'll set off. Did you come along this road to get here?'

'Yes, this one. And these pictures, what are they of? Is it the patrol?' he asked, dropping his voice in fear.

Matteo made no reply. All at once, thinking that he was returning to the house where he had believed he would never set foot again, his heart seemed to freeze. All his anguish, which for several minutes had receded into the background, rose and oppressed him. He forgot the little stranger he was carrying in his arms and thought: 'Why have I prolonged my agony?'

The child indistinctly understood that something in his friend had changed. He looked at him timidly, prey, too, to his own little thoughts. What was wrong with the gentleman holding him in his arms? Was he playing a trick on him? What if, instead of taking him to his house and giving him the books with the coloured pictures, he was handing him over to the patrol?

In his child's mind, that invisible squad of soldiers marching through the darkness in rhythmic step, accompanied by a mysterious clanking of sabres, contained something monstrous, more subtly terrifying than all the intangible fantasies of infancy.

'Where is the patrol now?' he asked in a stifled voice.

Matteo understood the working of the child's mind and

wanted to make use of it.

'I don't know where it is, but we might meet it at any moment, and if you don't tell me your name…'

'My name is Gino Lauretti.'

'Lauretti? I don't know anyone of that name,' thought Matteo, swiftly searching his memory, but not wishing to dwell on it for fear of losing this opportunity.

The boy shivered slightly. Matteo walked rapidly, beneath the moon, a little tired from the unaccustomed weight, and forgetful again of his own concerns.

'So you're called Gino Lauretti. Excellent. And your Papa is called Antonio?'

'No, he's called Andrea.'

'Ah, Andrea? And Mamma?'

'Mamma is dead.'

Matteo began to understand, if not altogether clearly. 'And your little brothers and sisters?'

'I don't have any, I don't have any,' the child said emphatically, pushing himself upright. His large eyes were shining. 'She says Lauretta is my sister, but it isn't true, it isn't true! She's horrible, is Lauretta, and she's another one who beats me too. I don't want her.'

Matteo listened intently, while keeping up his rapid pace.

Behind the child's words lay a whole sorry story. Who was "she"? The step-mother? He thought the best thing he could do was to let the little boy say everything he cared to, without interrupting him.

'When Papa's there, she doesn't say anything, or she laughs and says I'm naughty. And then Papa gets cross and tells me off and I get frightened and don't speak. Then when Papa has gone out, she starts to shout and says she's the mistress of the house, and beats me and shuts me away in the dark. I'm scared. Then she tells me: "Play with Lauretta, with your sister." But I don't want her. She scratches me, you know. And she says the snake is hers. I tell her: "You are the housekeeper's daughter, and I am Papa's son. I am the master." And she says: "And I am the mistress because my mother is in charge here." "No, you are the housekeeper's daughter, and the master is me." "But I am your sister." "You? You are nothing to me. Go away, go away, I can't see you, I don't want you." So then she scratches me, and then she shouts and says that I've scratched her. And then *she* comes, and she beats me, and locks me away where it's dark…'

'Who is "she"? Lauretta?'

'No, *she*, Luigina. Lauretta's mother.'

'Does she have a white apron?' Matteo asked, to ascertain whether this *she* was still the housekeeper or whether Gino's father had married her.

'She puts it on when there are people there.'

'Very good. And then?'

'And Papa went away the other day, and he said he'd be away for a few days. Then Lauretta said: "Now I'm the mistress". And she began to run about on all the chairs, hitting them with the whip, and she took my little horse and my little sheep. And I shouted at her: "I am the master, get down, piggy-eyes!" Then Lauretta slapped me and said: "She's the mistress, your father is leaving everything to her and to you, nothing. And now that he's not here, I'm locking you in the dark, on bread and water, and the dead bodies will come and get you, ugly toad." So then I thought of running away, of going to

Papa, of telling him everything, and I ran away. Then I was tired and I sat down and I fell asleep. And where is the patrol now?'

'Don't be afraid. It's a long way away. And now that you've told me everything, I won't call it any more.'

On entering his house, Matteo again experienced a dreadful moment of chill at the resurgence of all the mental anguish which had separated him from the rest of the world. He thought: 'I'll put a notice in the paper, I'll leave the boy in Maria's care and… it will all be over.'

The servant was already in bed; it was about nine o'clock.

Matteo turned up the lamp in his small study and opened the window, through which the moonlight flooded.

The child looked around him curiously; after a while he asked: 'But don't you have any children?'

Oh, no, he had no children; and Matteo thought with a start that if he had married in time and had had a child like Gino, things would have gone differently with him.

An unexpected wave of tenderness came over him.

'I must live until they come to fetch him, and it must be the father who comes, it has to be, otherwise I won't pass him over to anyone.'

'Where has your father gone?' he said aloud. 'Do you know, little friend?'

'To Rome.'

Every time the father went away, that was what Gino believed and repeated. Matteo ingenuously trusted the boy's answer.

'Perhaps it will be a while before he returns,' he thought. 'Very well, it means my pain must continue. But I'm not handing the boy over to anyone. It's essential the father knows, that he opens his eyes and protects him.'

He made the child sit at his desk and put a volume before him, a book of the brothers Grimm's tales, with illustrations in colour (it had been sent to him to review).

Gino was quiet, slowly turning the pages of the book.

Matteo took a sheet of paper and wrote a few lines, which he read through carefully, passing a hand over his hair.

"Found: a lost child, calling himself Gino Lauretti, son of Andrea. Any relatives should present themselves at number so-and-so, in so-and-so street, to collect him."

'It's as if one were dealing with a mere object,' Matteo thought, raising his head and folding the paper. Gino looked up as well.

'Why are you wearing glasses?' he asked.

'Because I can't see very much,' Matteo replied, laughing.

'Do you see more with glasses on? Let me try them.'

Matteo took them off and placed them on Gino.

'No, no, like this,' the child said, standing up and settling them on his nose again. 'Wait, look, look. Oh, that's wonderful!'

Matteo gazed at him with growing affection: old memories came back to him, like shining dots in a distant, long-forgotten past. The glasses flashed with reflections from the lamp, while in the magnified and laughing eyes of the child gleamed a charming ray of innocent mischief.

'Can you see?'

'I can see,' the child replied, who could indeed see, though everything was hazy. 'Look, is this funny old thing an orc?'

'It is an orc.'

There was a short silence. Gino removed the glasses and

asked, hesitantly: 'Are there still orcs?'

Matteo took the glasses, breathed on them, cleaned them carefully with the little cloth: and he understood that in making this remark the boy was thinking of a person he hated. He was in difficulties to know how to answer.

'Wait a moment,' he said, 'I'll be back very soon.'

'Where are you going?'

'I'm going to call the servant to go out and buy you some sweets.'

He left the room, holding the sheet of paper, and crossing the threshold he thought: 'Well anyway, what's the hurry? As long as the father's away. Why not leave it until tomorrow…? No, it's not right.'

He woke the servant and sent her to the offices of the newspaper where he meant to place the notice.

'Tell them to insert it in tonight's edition, quick, Maria.'

Returning to the study he heard the sounds of Gino up to some noisy prank. He looked in: with the light behind him, the little boy was prancing and gesticulating in front of the wall, laughing at the grotesque leaps and flourishes of his own shadow.

Matteo came into the room and sat down on the small divan, and taking the boy on his knee began a childish conversation with him.

The following day a woman, quite young and dressed with discreet elegance, came to claim the child. Matteo was waiting for her and when he saw her he examined her closely, supressing a kind of anger that simmered inside him.

'You are *signora* Luigina?'

'Yes, *signore*.'

Her features, despite the elegance of her dress and hair, gave her away as a servant.

'I'm sorry,' said Matteo, 'but I cannot hand the boy over to you. I can only hand him over to his father.'

'His father is absent.'

'We shall wait for him to return.'

She flushed with irritation.

'Excuse me, but you must let me have him, otherwise I shall take the matter to the authorities.'

'You would be better advised not to do that. You may come to regret it.'

'We shall see.'

'We shall see.'

She left, in a rage. Matteo remained at home all day, talking with the young boy, who quickly made friends with the maid as well.

Gino made no mention of leaving; on the contrary, he seemed to have completely forgotten the reason for his original flight. With Matteo he was calm and composed, a little timid, looking at everything with great curiosity and asking him for explanations, but never touching anything.

Every so often, however, he started, alert and listening, as if he heard noises in the distance. Observing him closely, Matteo realised that those little shivers, those moments of fear and anxiety, were recollections of horrors already suffered.

'Ah,' he told himself from time to time, 'that woman's not going to steal him away, no, she'll not get her hands on him!'

She did not return again that day. Next day, she did come, alone.

'All alone? How's that?' Matteo asked ironically.

She did not deign to reply, but produced a telegram from the master, which requested Matteo to hand the child over to her.

Matteo looked to see where the telegram had been sent from and saw the name of a city close by.

'What's this?' he thought. 'He's not in Rome? Well, all the better.'

'The *signora* will forgive me,' he said to Luigina, handing back the telegram, 'but I remain firm in my resolve and you may do whatever you please.'

Then she began to assault his ears with the coarsest of words, her voice shrill; and her face, which was quite pretty, took on a vulgar, almost repellent, expression. Matteo let her rail at him, staring at her with deep distaste. He could imagine all the torments this awful woman must have put the child through, and he wondered what kind of man this Lauretti must be to allow himself to be dominated by such a vulgar mistress.

'Don't shout quite so loudly, *signora*,' he said, with ironic courtesy. 'Remember, those who make most noise are usually in the wrong. I repeat, you can do what you please, but I shall not give the child over to anyone except the father in person. To hasten his return, I will write to him today. I'll do it now, and inform him of everything that has been going on.'

She fell silent, evidently unnerved by these last words.

'Do what you like,' she said, trying to appear cool, and she went away.

Matteo wrote a long letter to Lauretti, noticeably severe in tone. It openly criticised his behaviour and told him he was not a good man and that henceforth the care of this young person should be placed in the hands of others.

These words, however, written without reflection, brought back to him that frozen sensation, that emptiness, which assailed him when he thought about his imminent end.

Ah, he was going to die: who could keep the boy safe then?

He stayed in the house all that day as well, in the company of the charming Gino. The hours flew swiftly by, almost serenely, in a misty denial of his fate.

Towards evening a letter from Luigina was brought to him. The woman, fearful of what might happen if the full truth was revealed to the master, had now turned humble and imploring. She begged him not to compromise her, promising from now on to shower the young runaway with affection.

Matteo became thoughtful: 'Supposing I believed her? Supposing I washed my hands of all this? What could I expect? What should I do?'

'What should I do?' he immediately asked himself again. He remembered that he was supposed to die. And in that moment he experienced a sensation, not exactly new, but only felt once before, in the first few days after the idea of suicide had crept into his mind. He felt, that is, a mysterious fear of death. It seemed that the courage one needed to die had somehow ebbed a little. He became aware of this fear, examined it, and felt a surge of anger.

'Ah, I've allowed time to slip by!' he exclaimed to himself. 'One more day and I'll die like the coward I am.'

And once again he considered the idea of granting the young woman's wish and handing the child over to her before Lauretti returned.

He took a visiting card, scribbled two or three lines, read

them through closely as was his custom. Then suddenly he leapt to his feet, tore the card into pieces and went to look for the boy. A strange new idea had come to him.

'Perhaps that child is more of a nuisance to his father than anything else. I'll make him a proposition: I'll offer to let him leave the boy here with me; I'll adopt him; I'll make him my heir.'

At this idea, the vision of death receded into the distance.

In the night that followed, Matteo was unable to sleep. His new vision seemed ever simpler, and vague plans for the future began to occupy his thoughts.

The past retreated into the background. The vast griefs which had sowed in his mind the seeds of suicide became small ones, no more than hazily perceived. On the contrary, at times Matteo found himself secretly marvelling how he had ever decided to die.

The weather remained continuously beautiful and spring-like, and this reinforced Matteo's new feelings. In the evenings, when he went out on the balcony with little Gino, the great diaphanous sky, with a brilliant Venus setting towards the horizon, and then the pale blue dusk with a luminous moon swimming in it, and the tepid air suffused with strange voices and the vibrations of distant sounds, and then the humid scent of the white chrysanthemums on the balcony glowing like moons, all this filled him with a sorrowing tenderness, a feeling almost sentimental, and palpitating with life.

He felt that life had mysteriously attached itself to the threads of a dream, and that this dream was absurd: yet he continued to dream it, and thus dreaming, he seemed to be suspended between life and death.

The child appeared to be happy. He had taken possession of the whole apartment, extending to every object his exhaustive curiosity and accepting the explanations, clear or otherwise, of Matteo and the maidservant.

In the four days that had passed, he had not cried once, nor asked either to go or to stay. He seemed to possess, to an extraordinary degree, the virtue of adaptability, and to enjoy without thinking the present moment. He knew that his father must come to collect him very soon, but he did not fear his arrival.

Matteo became ever more convinced that the little boy must have suffered dreadful mistreatment if, by nature as calm as this, as patient and as polite, he had run away from home.

What was he thinking all this time?

'Your father is coming,' Matteo told him. 'Tomorrow, or maybe today. He's coming and he's taking you with him.'

'And where is he taking me?'

'Why, home! With Lauretta.'

'No, he'll leave me here,' Gino said tranquilly.

The same dream as Matteo's, then, had established itself in that little soul as well, and soothed all his former agitation.

It gave Matteo a strange sense of joy, a happy presentiment of good things. He had only to wait for Lauretti. Every time someone knocked at the door, Matteo felt his heart beat violently and his face changed colour.

Lauretti, however, did not appear until two days later. He was a tall, thin man, with deep-set blue eyes and an unwavering gaze. A drooping yellowish moustache cut across his pasty features. A brutish-looking type, who immediately filled Matteo with repugnance.

Matteo had himself turned pale on receiving him. Lauretti promptly apologised for not being able to come sooner. His voice was low-pitched and coarse, his words halting. He seemed a man lacking in sensibility or force of will; and Matteo hoped more than ever to see his desire granted.

Lauretti continued to make his excuses. 'In any case,' he said, 'you could have handed the child over to the housekeeper. There was no need to put yourself to all this trouble.'

'What?' Matteo said, amazed, and almost offended. 'Did you not receive my letter then?'

'To be sure,' the man replied, putting a hand to his overcoat pocket as if to indicate the letter was there.

'But in that case, excuse me, how can you say I could have handed the child over to the housekeeper?'

'Why, to save yourself all this trouble.'

'Excuse me,' Matteo said, becoming excited, 'either I'm deceiving myself or you have not understood the seriousness of the situation.'

'I understand perfectly well, but what do you expect me to say about it? Perhaps the child is exaggerating… In any event, it won't happen again.'

'What? What? The child is exaggerating? But if you don't trust the word of an innocent creature…'

A dozen fiery retorts sprang to Matteo's lips, but he held them back in order not to give offence to the vile man who stood before him, and not to damage his cause, his dream. He sat down in sad disarray and allowed Laurettit to talk on, but paid no attention to what he was saying. Then he told him: 'Very well, you are his father and you can see better than I what needs to be done.' (That was the wrong thing to say, he instantly thought, I shouldn't have put it like that.) 'With your permission, I…' (No, permission was a mistake: I need to impose myself and make my proposal more appealing, he added mentally.) 'If you'll allow me to do you a favour, I'd like to make you a proposition.'

'Go on.'

'Listen then: I have no family, I am not without means. Over the last few days I've become very fond of the child. If you think it suitable, I will keep him here with me, I will adopt him, I will make him my heir.'

Lauretti flushed a little and didn't speak for a moment. In that ugly reddening, in that rather heavy silence, Matteo could sense the man's condemnation.

'I thank you for your kind offer, but the idea is impossible. That boy is my only child: what would people say?'

Matteo realised that in speaking this way Lauretti had his mistress in mind. He knew she must have persuaded him to smooth over the scandal at all costs, and Lauretti was aware that Matteo could read his thoughts. They exchanged a swift glance of loathing.

'So it's no use my urging you to think again?' Matteo said. 'You should consider this: the child wishes to stay with me. As for what people would say, they wouldn't say anything. Besides, tongues will wag anyway over certain less noble affairs.' (Lauretti felt the thrust go deep.) 'Why shouldn't we let tongues wag over this as well?'

'It's no good. I can't.'

'For the moment?'

'For the moment and for always,' Lauretti responded with a firmness one would have thought beyond him.

Matteo felt his spirits droop; but all at once something rose again in the depths of his soul and blazed in his eyes. His features became severe and menacing, his voice hard.

'Very well,' he said, standing up, 'take the child. Restore him to his own home. Let him live alongside that woman. But be aware: if she doesn't know how to treat him, there are others who do know.'

Lauretti stood up also, without replying, without taking offence. To confound him, and to convince him, Matteo showed him the letter from Luigina. The man read it with interest, but then observed: 'It's clear enough that she too promises to treat the boy well from now on.'

A feeling of hopeless disgust came over Matteo, but all his contempt and anger fell away before this man, who was perhaps more a pathetic wretch than a villain.

'Let the child have his lunch here with me, for today, 'he said. 'I'll bring him back to your house myself.'

'It will be better that way, yes, thank you,' the other said, inclining his head.

'And you will at least allow me to see him often?'

'And keep an eye on him as well,' Lauretti said with a laugh, making his way towards the door.

And Matteo forced himself to laugh too, and murmured in confusion: 'That as well… that as well…'

On the threshold they coldly touched hands. Lauretti gave another little bow, thanked him again and went calmly on his way.

Then Matteo went into the child's room, lifted him on to his lap and contemplated him for several minutes; and something happened that had not happened to him since his own childhood: two tears rolled down his cheeks.

The child looked at him, half in wonder, half in alarm.

'Has someone you know died?' he asked timidly, very quietly.

No, no one he knew had died. On the contrary, someone had come back to life: himself. Whether the child lived with his father or with him, the bond he had dreamed of making with the boy would never be broken.

TWO KINDS OF JUSTICE

In a poor Sardinian village the poorest inhabitant was Quirico
Oroveru. He went by the nickname Barabbas, having once
represented this character in a religious pageant.

Uncle Chircu Barabbas was even poorer than the beggars.
He owned one shirt, one pair of canvas trousers, a pair of
woollen drawers and a cap made by himself from the pelt of a
hare. He had no buttons on his shirt, no coat, no overcoat, no
gaiters. He did not even have shoes, the height of wretchedness
for a man from those parts.

Nevertheless he was healthy and strong, a fine figure with
something of the Celt about him. He was tall and ruddy, with
eyes that were always smiling. But it was only to be expected:
he had been brought up this way. Gathering wood in the forest
and selling it was the only life he knew. As for anything else,
he was as harmless as a lizard and as innocent as a child of

seven. The only things he owned, apart from the clothes, were a silver medallion which had hung round his neck since he was a boy, an axe, a horse-hair rope woven by his own hand and a clasp knife.

And yet he was mostly quite content, and certainly more at peace than *signor* Saturnino Solitta, the richest man in the district. This gentleman lived in a spacious new house, so white it seemed to be made of blocks of snow, its glittering windows reflecting the blue of the sky.

Uncle Chircu spent almost all his days in the forest. He found it silent and beautiful whatever the season or time of day, whether the holm-oaks were covered in the pale gold flowers of spring or the blue afternoons of summer bore down overhead. He loved it when a damp green hush prevailed under a silvery autumn sky or when the great boughs bent under their burden of frost-crystallised snow. The woodcutter's axe never ceased. The trees would continuously echo the hatchet's blow — *tock, tock, tock. Kee-yew, kee-yew, kee-yew* — would come the distant reply of a woodland bird from beside the green fountain. Nothing else stirred. Uncle Chircu would either pray, or think about which house would pay him best for bringing them firewood, or else he would dream about buying himself a pair of shoes.

One day, when he was about forty-five, two men dressed in dark blue with yellow buttons on their jackets accosted him in the forest.

'What are you doing?' they asked him.

'Can't you see?' he said, standing solidly, back bent beneath his burden of firewood but looking them squarely in the face.

'Do you own a parcel of land in this forest?'

He started to laugh, shifting a leg forward and looking down at one of his bare feet: 'I don't even have shoes.'

'Well then, you are in contravention of forestry regulations. Or who has given you permission to cut wood in the forest?'

'No one. I take it because if I didn't I'd starve.'

'Well then, you are in contravention of forestry regulations.'

'What does that mean?'

'It means you must pay a fine or go to prison.'

Uncle Chircu no longer felt inclined to laugh; rather the reverse. A cloud fell across his face.

'But I've been cutting wood here for thirty years and no one's ever told me I had to leave off and let myself die of hunger.'

The two forest keepers seemed touched.

'Well, that's how it is, my friend. That's the law now, and it has to be respected. On this occasion, you may go. But mind we don't catch you doing it again.'

Instead, they caught him doing it several times, and in the end, one day, they confiscated his load of firewood and declared him in contravention of the law. They were not bad men. On the contrary, they felt sympathy for the poor fellow, but what were they to do? It was their duty to uphold the law.

Uncle Chircu kept on with his wood cutting all the same, but took much greater precautions. He went deeper into the forest, to places where not even the *kee-yew, kew-yew* of the woodland bird carried. And the *tock, tock* of his axe striking a tree itself sounded timid, irregular. It was as if the trembling tree every now and then fell silent, listening fearfully. The due

47

processes of the law, meanwhile, had been put in motion and Uncle Chircu was summoned before the local magistrate. He was given a heavy fine, because all the witnesses, the owners of the forest, declared that he was one of the biggest and most persistent destroyers of the woods.

He would have to pay his debt to society by going to prison. It felt like a horrible dream, and he suffered as he had never suffered in all his life. Within a few days he seemed to have aged ten years. He became even dirtier and more tattered than before, and his eyes grew dull. No, no, he did not want to go to prison, at least in this fine summer weather. And he would not have wanted to be there even in the bad weather, because it was in winter that his wood was easy to sell. In the event, he came to an agreement with another man from his village and made off into the countryside. He was well enough accustomed to it after all, and it was of little importance to him where he stayed. He cut the firewood and the other man sold it, carrying it back to the village. But he swindled him out of half the profits and Chircu had no choice but to remain silent and accept it.

He felt deeply unhappy. He had to retreat to other stretches of forest a good distance away and for the most part he cut his logs by night, when the moon gleamed low over the lonely woodlands. The *tock, tock* of the axe in this strange lunar silence was answered now by the voice of the cuckoo, which seemed alternately to spring either from the depths of the woods or from the pale and gauzy heavens.

In this way the autumn passed. Winter passed too, and spring came. Uncle Chircu's wretched state had become extreme. He was almost naked, his hair and beard were wild and he was often starving. But he still did not want to give himself up. No, no, he had not given way all through the harsh chills of winter, and he was even less willing to surrender now that the sun was lending its faint warmth to the woodland clearings, newly fragrant with cyclamen and violets. He would give himself up when winter came again: there was still time.

Meanwhile, one day when he was crossing a stretch of flat country to move from one wooded area to another, fortune seemed to smile on him. Half hidden under a bush he found a large red pocket-book, two purses, a small pouch and some cards which the dew had somewhat dampened. He looked: there was no money but the cards must have been important and perhaps the owner would give a tip to anyone who restored them to him. So he gathered everything up and continued on his way, and when he next saw the friend who sold the wood for him, a man who could read, he told him all about it.

'Oh, Satan preserve us, those things belonged to *signor* Saturnino Solitta!' his companion cried, eyeing him suspiciously. A shudder of fear, of horror, went through Uncle Chircu. *Signor* Saturnino Solitta had been murdered not long before, on his way back from Cagliari where he had transported and sold a large number of fattened pigs. It was clear that the murderer, having taken the money, had thrown away the bags and cards.

'These are bills of exchange, and this piece of paper is a kind of money, look,' said the man from his village, who could read and write and had been a servant in a rich man's house. 'If you go into a shop they'll cash it for you straightaway. It's called a cheque.'

'But I don't want to do that. They'll think I was the one

who killed him.'

'Come on, you'd be an idiot not to go. After a few months, who do you think is going to remember anything about it in Nuoro? You go into town, as if you were a servant, make a few purchases, pocket the rest and calmly come away.'

'But… isn't that a kind of theft?'

'You're an idiot, devil take your hide! What kind of theft is it if the owner's no longer alive? The theft was committed by whoever put a bullet in his neck. Provided it wasn't you…'

'Oh, go to hell!' Uncle Chircu said, laughing so sincerely it completely ruled out his companion's strange idea.

'So why shouldn't you change this bit of paper? If nothing else, you can just say you found it… I would, I'm sure. Are you a complete ignoramus? Can't you see, you haven't a single item of clothing in one piece?'

'Ah, that's true! But that's just it, that's the thing. Wouldn't they distrust me if they saw me looking as ragged as this? In any case, after everything you've said, I'm not sure it matters to me anyway.'

'Well then, I'll lend you my shoes, my overcoat, my gaiters.'

'And your coat and hat as well?'

'You mean you want everything I've got on?'

'If you'll let me have it.'

'But… if I do… a little something…'

'Understood, I'll buy something for you. What would you like me to get?'

'Anything you like.'

For a while Uncle Chircu felt less unhappy than before.

He thought of all the fine things he could buy: boots,

clothes, a new axe. And he could buy things to eat, bread, bacon, wine. Deep down he experienced certain scruples, and a degree of fear. But after all, he had taken nothing, he had simply found it. And if necessary, he innocently believed it would be enough simply to tell the truth to extricate himself from any trouble. Every time his companion came to take away the firewood he urged him on, and on one occasion even went as far as to say that if he was scared he would go himself.

But mindful of how he had been swindled over the wood, Uncle Chircu was reluctant to trust him and preferred to go to Nuoro himself.

He went straightaway to buy a pair of boots in yellow leather, with long black laces and hobnails so big they looked like silver studs. He tried them on for size, pulled the laces tight, slackened them off, and put on his friend's shoes again, which painfully squeezed his enormous black feet. And with a beating heart he pulled from his belt the dead man's cheque. The shopkeeper took it, examined it. Not a muscle moved in his face. But in that moment he decided the fate of poor Uncle Barabbas.

'I don't have any change,' he said. 'But if you wait a moment, I'll send round to my neighbour's shop next door and have this cashed.'

Uncle Chircu felt slightly anxious, but let him do so.

In the meantime he considered whether to take off his friend's shoes once more and put on the new boots, more comfortable, if a little too heavy.

'They're as hard as the devil's hide,' he thought, bending down and testing them with his fingers. 'But we'll rub a little grease into them and they'll soon get softer. They're beautiful boots, really beautiful!'

The man sent by the shopkeeper to cash the cheque was a long time coming back. The shopkeeper, anxious and nervous, strode to the doorway at intervals and looked out. Eventually the man returned. Immediately behind him came a well-dressed gentleman with plump and ruddy lips, and entering the shop behind this gentleman came two policemen. Uncle Chircu felt his heart turn cold: he sensed what was about to happen, and for a moment he was afraid. But almost at once he thought: 'I'll tell the truth, and everything will be all right.'

All this happened very quickly.

'Who gave you this cheque?' the gentleman with the plump lips asked.

'I found it,' Uncle Chircu replied respectfully, standing up straight and holding his friend's shoes in his hand.

'Where did you find it?'

'Round and about.'

'My good man,' said the gentleman in a friendly sort of manner, possibly fearing this tall and wild-looking man could make trouble, 'you must do me the kindness of coming with us to explain the matter more clearly to the Inspector.'

And Uncle Chircu followed them docilely, carrying in his heart the delusion that it was sufficient to tell the truth to be believed. But in the depths of his soul he could feel a mysterious sense of oppression, the secret presentiment of something terrible.

In the office, the manner of the gentleman and the policemen changed. Uncle Chircu was interrogated again, this time roughly, by another gentleman, pale and bald. Then he was stripped and searched. They found the spoils of the crime on him, and he was promptly held for the murder of *signor* Saturnino Solitta.

They threw him in jail, they subjected him to long, cruel, horrible interrogations. Every day different gentlemen came, this one with spectacles, this one with a blond beard, and they asked him a barrage of strange questions. What they wanted above all was for him to tell them how and when he had murdered *signor* Saturnino Solitta.

'But I haven't murdered anyone,' he kept on saying. 'These things, I just found them, and I didn't even know what they were. A friend advised me to exchange this piece of paper and since I badly wanted a pair of shoes I followed his advice. Ask him, if you don't believe me.'

They brought him in, they asked him. The man admitted lending his clothes — and he wanted them back — and lending his shoes to Oroveru, but he knew nothing, he had advised nothing.

'What a scoundrel, what a brazen face,' Chircu told himself. 'Ah! Really! I should have thought of that, after the business with the firewood!'

'Well,' he said to the judge, to avenge himself, 'if he didn't advise me in any way, he didn't lend me his clothes either.' That way, at least they won't return them, he thought. But then he repented and took his words back. Ah, no, he didn't wish to offer further offence to God's goodness, certain as he was that this present disgrace was happening to him because he had already sinned in appropriating another man's belongings.

He felt deeply miserable through the long hours locked in a cell, instinctively yearning for the great solitary forests and the open sky. He remembered the days when he had been a fugitive from justice and how harshly he had suffered. He thought he had sinned by feeling sorry for himself then, because the hardships of those days had been a great happiness compared to this present wretchedness. And yet he still had no idea of the terrible things that awaited him.

He kept hoping at any moment to be set free, and every night, as he fell asleep, he could hear the *tock, tock* of the axe echoing in the silence of the forest, accompanied by the slow and melancholy call of the cuckoo.

A long time went by. No one remembered Uncle Barabbas. No one had any converse with him, as the expression goes, or sent him a cigar or a litre of wine or a loaf of fresh bread or a clean shirt, although even the poorest of the prisoners received such things. Even those gentlemen with the shiny spectacles that made you tremble to look at them, or with blond beards, or pale and bald, had forgotten about him.

But one day they sent him a document, part of it printed, part handwritten. Fearfully, he had it explained to him. It was the decision of the local justices, remanding him for trial at the Assizes. Then they sent him a lawyer, a youth with a greenish face who switched from bad temper to indifference minute by minute. This youth also demanded that Uncle Chircu admit he had murdered *signor* Saturnino Solitta.

'Tell me the truth,' he said. 'You have to confess the whole truth to your lawyer, and then things can be settled.'

For an instant Uncle Barabbas was tempted to say that he had murdered Solitta. It seemed so much easier to escape his predicament by confessing to the supposed crime than by stating the truth. But when he was no longer confronted by the lawyer's greenish features, his mind rebelled and he placed

54

his hope again in the triumph of truth. And then, his fellow prisoners told him that jurymen were upright, honest people, with human hearts and not hearts of stone like the magistrates'.

The day of the trial came. Uncle Chircu woke almost happy. He had dreamed he was in the woods, cutting logs, beside a stream. On a branch of overgrown willow, a marsh bird, black, with long green legs and toes like reeds, was singing a strange song.

Among those who appeared as witnesses was his friendly wood-cutting assistant, and there were others, who testified to the defendant's being a rough and uncivilised man, taciturn, unsociable.

The public prosecutor depicted him as 'a feral creature of the forests, who had long planned this crime, lying in wait for his victim like a wild beast waiting for the opportunity to pounce on his prey.' Quite so.

Uncle Barabbas stared in alarm at this gentleman in the shiny spectacles, a man to whom he had never done any harm, and experienced a strange feeling of terror.

He turned his gaze on the jury for reassurance. They were men from the surrounding villages, stout, pacific, humane-looking men; and he hoped. The lawyer spoke. His face seemed greener than ever. What little élan he could summon amounted only to baring his lips and clashing his teeth, which had the most undesirable of effects.

It was enough. The poor man was condemned to forced labour for life. He wept bitterly. He looked again at the jury, those stout, pacific, fair-minded looking men. He remembered his dream, his blind faith that truth would triumph, and he told himself that all the things that seemed beautiful were false.

To comfort him, the lawyer told him they could have prompt recourse to the Court of Appeal. But he no longer had any faith, he did not believe, held out no more hopes. His heart tightened, became dry and bitter like the shrivelled fruits of a wild plum tree. He no longer prayed, he no longer wept.

And they took him away, far, far away, to a salt-marsh. They shaved off his hair, his beard, his moustache. They dressed him in a red suit and soldered a chain round his foot. For the first weeks and months he lived in despair: the immense vista of the sea, to a man accustomed to moist, enclosed woodlands, only increased his sense of hopeless nostalgia.

But with the passing of the years he grew accustomed to everything, he became resigned, and his memories grew confused. Sometimes indeed, thinking that if he had remained free his old age would have been one of blackest misery, he took comfort from knowing that his future was now secure.

However, he had become bad: he had lost the innocence he had preserved until the day of his sentencing. He swore, and if the opportunity arose, he stole and got drunk like the vilest of his fellow convicts. He never thought about God any more, or if he did it was with anger, as a monstrous being who had permitted the most disgraceful injustice to be visited on one of his creatures.

Among his companions in misfortune, Uncle Barabbas struck up a friendship with another Sardinian, a little old man who hardly came up to his waist, and in whose red and chubby little face shone two deep-set eyes of the most vivid blue.

He was a native of a district not far from Uncle Chircu's; his name was Pietro but he was known in his village as Uncle Pretu.

He was a cheerful little man, free-thinking and equally free with the truth. When he had persuaded his fellow prisoners to believe all manner of marvels, he would laugh coarsely, however, saying his stories were all fantasies. By the time Uncle Chircu arrived at the penal settlement, no one any longer believed a word Uncle Pretu said. If he did say anything true, though, his manner was different and impressed itself on the listener. But Uncle Pretu rarely uttered such truths, and to very few people. With that rare accent of truth, and in few words, he told Uncle Chircu his story once he had gained his trust.

'Listen. I'm from so-and-so district. I was doing well, you know, I had cows, beehives, fields sown with grain and beans. But I wanted to do better. I knew there was a wealthy priest who even had gold knives and forks, a whole table service, and with a few companions we went along to steal it. He started yelling so we grabbed him by the throat and he ended up dead. Along came the law, just at the wrong moment: bang, bang, shots here, shots there, shots everywhere. We had to run, but one of our people was caught by the soldiers and he revealed our names, the coward. Which meant I had to take to the hills, and to stop the law from appropriating my property, I sold the lot within the first few days. I shoved the money in a metal box and I buried it. Then I was caught.'

'And the loot?' Uncle Chircu asked.

'Ah, I used that to keep me fed while I was on the run. But I can tell you, they were sour mouthfuls, those were,' the old man replied, launching a gob of spittle into the distance. Then he asked: 'And what's your story?'

'Oh,' said the other bitterly, 'I've robbed a man too and

killed him, like you. The only difference is they laid these crimes on me, but I didn't actually do them.'

'Ah, that is unjust. I really did kill him, there's no denying it. And I've been forced to regret it, because in the end I've lost everything.'

'But don't you have any family?' Uncle Chircu asked, thinking of the buried box.

'Family be damned! They abandoned me like a dog. I hope they're living like dogs now too.'

In this way Uncle Chircu and Uncle Pietro struck up their friendship, which lasted through long years and became in some ways a consolation to the two miserable fellows. Rather than companions in arms they were companions in chains, they came from the same place: they often spoke of their distant homeland. And they were also united in the conviction that they must both die down here, mere numbers lost in the white desolation of the salt-marshes built by the sea and the sun.

Uncle Chircu was often snarling and provocative, his character having completely changed. In certain moments when he was in a black mood he insulted his elderly companion and came close to striking him. Then the little old man would start to laugh and tell him: 'You Nobody, if you carry on acting bad, I won't tell you where my box is hidden.'

The other would become even angrier.

'Devil take your hide, even if you did tell me, what makes you think you'd be doing me a favour?'

'If nothing else, you'll know as well.'

'I hope the devil gets his spurs into you, I hope the devil pickles you in brine, don't make me even angrier, you Nobody.'

When they called each other Nobody instead of using

their name, it was the worst insult they could exchange.

One day when he was in a good mood, Uncle Chircu said to his companion while they were doing their work out on the salt-marsh: 'Well, why don't you write to someone, then they can dig up the box and send you some money? You could make life easier for yourself, buy a bit of this, a bit of that.'

'Rubbish! They'd keep the lot. I know people better than you do.'

'But in that case, what...?'

'Well, what? I know what you're getting at. Well, I'll tell a poor man where it is, on my death-bed. Yes, someone really poor. Then he can have prayers said for my soul.'

And the days, the months, the years went by.

Uncle Chircu's hair turned grey, his chest hollow, his height diminished. Uncle Pretu was almost worn out with age, but he didn't seem any older than his companion and continued to tell tall stories and laugh at them. It was as if he recounted his follies, with wearying humour, more to entertain himself than anyone else.

Finally, one day something extraordinary happened. Uncle Chircu was summoned before the director of the penal settlement. He made his way there somewhat bewildered. Nothing similar had ever happened to him before. The director said: 'So many years have passed by now, you are an old man and you can finally tell the truth. Did you, yes or no, commit the crime? Tell the truth, the whole truth. It will be to your advantage: we will ask for a pardon, and it could be that you can go and die in your own country.'

Uncle Chircu denied it once more, with savage energy.

'No, even if I were to live as many years as there are

grains of sand in the sea and I had to live them out here, no. I have not murdered anyone. No, no and no.'

He was taken away. When he saw Uncle Pretu again — who was waiting anxiously — he told him wrathfully what had happened.

'Ah, the devil,' the old man said. 'The whole thing is unjust. I really did kill the priest, there's no two ways about it, and if they call me in I'll confess it again, and if they want to pardon me they certainly can. But to torment a poor devil like you, oh, that's not right!'

Uncle Chircu was called to see the director for a second time the following day and was interrogated all over again.

He felt the blood rise to his head. Any more of this and he would have hurled himself at the director, so little did he have to lose by this time.

'Well, since that's the way it is,' said the director, his tone changing, 'I can tell you that the real culprit has been found. Or more accurately, he hasn't been found, he was overcome by remorse and he's given himself up and confessed, but it comes to the same thing. So you can prepare yourself with a clear mind, because in a short while you'll be free.'

And he was taken away again. He went out trembling, and when he rejoined Uncle Pretu he began to cry in a way his companion had never seen him do before.

'Well then, well then? What's happened?'

'The real culprit has been found,' Uncle Chircu replied, sobbing and repeating the director's own words. 'Or more accurately he hasn't been found, he was overcome by remorse and he's given himself up and confessed, but it comes to the same thing. I have to prepare myself to be free.'

Uncle Pretu began to cry as well. The pair of them wept out of grief and joy, fused into a single emotion.

'How am I going to manage?' Uncle Pretu asked.

'And how am I going to manage?' said Uncle Chircu. 'Freedom is a fine thing, and then I'll have my good reputation back. But I'm an old man now, I won't be able to work any more, I won't be able to live, I don't have anybody.'

'They will give you something.'

'Ah, no, that's not for me: I don't want charity. Why don't you tell me where your box is?' he then said, with a sad smile and a touch of irony.

Uncle Pretu's face lit up.

'Well, yes, why not? You're a poor man. All right, yes, I'll tell you. I'd already thought of it. But you must remember me in your prayers.'

'Ah, I can't remember any of my prayers!' Uncle Chircu exclaimed, stricken. 'I have forgotten God, but God has not forgotten me. God has only been testing me, but I have been living like a Hebrew.'

On the day of his departure, Uncle Pretu told him where his box was hidden. They parted sadly: for Uncle Pretu this was the final sorrow, but the old man found a degree of consolation in thinking that, before he died, he could do some good to a poor fellow on whom God had laid a heavy hand. Uncle Chircu also parted calm in his mind, thinking of his restored reputation and his assured future.

When he was back in his old surroundings again, everyone was kind and charitable, providing him with enough to live on for a while. He thought continuously of the old convict's hidden box, but he couldn't yet stir himself to go and find it because

he felt weak, incapable of making a long journey. He needed to regain his strength first. In the first few weeks after his
return he received many gifts and demonstrations of affection.
But gradually the people of the district grew used to seeing
him, they stopped thinking about him and they forgot him.

So then he set out on his journey and went to look for
the crock of gold. His heart beat fiercely as he recognised
the places where he had lived before his disgrace. Many of
the woods had been thinned out; a few had been completely
levelled. But among the elders along the brook there still
sounded the *kee-yew*, *kee-yew* of the marsh birds, from the
thickets of lentisk rose the slow and even note of the cuckoo,
and those voices brought back to old Barabbas many things.

A curious melancholy seized him. He thought how he had
become bad since those distant days, and how he had despaired
of divine mercy. He thought of Uncle Pretu and could not help
wondering if he, a man who had indeed committed a crime and
was expiating it with resignation and acts of goodness, was not
a better man than himself.

Ah, no, it was not possible that he should find the treasure.
He did not deserve it, for he had sinned too gravely, despaired
too violently! Then he repented of this new despair, and he
prayed and continued on his way with more vigour.

He arrived towards evening at the place indicated by
the old convict. It was a small wood of poplars in a deserted
location some distance from any inhabited area. As darkness
gathered, brilliant stars began to appear in the purest of skies.
The poplars thrust into the air, their long trunks sharply
defined, their tops like enormous silvery flowers. From the
soft leaf-strewn earth rose a vague damp fragrance.

Uncle Barabbas had brought the head of a small mattock with him. He pulled it from under his coat and rummaged through the leaves for some time to find a branch that would make a handle of some sort, and fitted it. Then he waited for the moon to rise. Meanwhile his heart beat rapidly: the rest of his days were at stake. Without divine assistance, he would spend them destitute and forgotten. He sat on the ground and covered his face with his hands.

Oh, how he had sinned! But he repented it all bitterly, and felt that even if he did not find the box, he would not complain, acknowledging his failure as God's just punishment.

The moon came up. The leaves of the poplars, bathed in its light, glowed like silver; the damp smell became sharper.

Uncle Barabbas levered himself to his knees and began to dig, fearful of the only sound in all that infinite, solitary silence, the sound made by his own digging. The earth was damp and black. It came loose easily, spilling over the knees of the old man whose back bent ever lower. Eventually the little mattock made a metallic sound, as it met a solid object. Uncle Barabbas reached his arm down, touched the handle of the box. Then he began to dig with furious energy, and soon the box was out. He shook it. Jingle, jingle, jingle went the coins inside.

Then he made the sign of the cross, and with his face raised towards the heavens he gave thanks for God's mercy.

He looked like a mad old man adoring the moon.

THE BLACK MARE

Sending two servants on ahead, Antonio Dalvy was going from village to village acquiring mares and foals of good stock to send to the mainland. He was a handsome man in his forties, tall, stout, and he carried his head high. His eyes, slightly slanting, slightly greenish, burned with an intensity which his drooping eyelids only partly concealed. He was discreetly wealthy, married to a noble wife, industrious and altogether held in high esteem.

He was a substantial trader in products such as bark, charcoal and clinker, and each year he made a trip to the mainland for orders. That year, one of his contacts had asked him to acquire a certain number of foals and mares, stock of good quality, in Sardinia. Anticipating a good profit, he had promptly set to work.

Accompanying him, or going on ahead, the two assistants,

Bellia and Ghisparru, were scouring the villages and countryside round Nuoro for good-looking foals with perfect conformation, and mares with melancholy eyes.

This is the way his deals were done: Dalvy would pay the seller a deposit, in the presence of two witnesses, and leave the selected animals in his charge. When they returned, having completed their tour, master and servants would pass by again to collect the foals and mares, paying the balance of the price.

Dalvy made his rounds astride a fine chestnut horse, a noble animal given to tossing its rather small head. It was May. When the sun shone hotly, when the tall grasses of the open plains gleamed motionless beneath the splendour of an azure sky, the merchant would open a green umbrella and fix it in front of him to shade his face.

Then the oblique line of his half-closed eyes, under the green shade and in the green reflections from the meadows and woods, would glow like a flash of emerald: it was quite discernible even from a distance.

One day, the two assistants came upon a church standing isolated in the countryside.

'Let's go and say a Hail Mary,' said Ghisparru, who was a devout sort of man even if ignorant and wild-looking.

But Bellia had been a soldier and had no great belief in God. He laughed at his companion's proposal.

All the same, they made their way up to the church. It was a very small church, and it rose from within two courtyards, one inside the other, both of them lined with little rooms or stalls, known locally as *cumbissias*. The more devout of the inhabitants of the neighbouring towns and villages would come here and live in them at the time of the *novena*.

Now, the little church with its two courtyards, its two entrance gates, its two circles of *cumbissias*, lay deserted and silent among the green fields and the wild flora of the heath. Inside was another heath in miniature, dense with clumps of bushes, sweet briars, flowering myrtles and arbutus.

Distant grasslands, pastures, rows of corn formed the horizon. A thread of water, running between elders and tamarisks, glittered far off.

Swallows flashed past, whistling like darts from one set of church railings to another. And sitting in the shade of the first gateway, an old warden was weaving a bunch of reeds.

The two servants approached, crossed themselves and greeted the warden.

The old man returned their greeting without getting up or pausing in his work.

'What church is this?' Ghisparru asked, bending his large and shaggy grey head and peering through the two open gates, outer and inner, with interest.

'Saint John the Baptist, brother of God,' the warden replied, making the sign of the cross.

'Will you show it to us?'

'And why not?'

The old man got to his feet, carefully setting down the bundles of green reeds, the cool smell of the marshes still on them, and led the two men into the church.

It was quite an impressive church, and probably a wealthy one, with its marble flooring and altar, and a number of frescoes, somewhat roughly executed, in which God appeared as a very old man with a large white beard, seated on clouds.

On the altar, a charming, fair-haired Saint John, dressed

like a Sardinian in sheep skins, offered a smiling blessing.

The three men genuflected, then inspected the church's cool, clean and bright interior.

The swallows swooped rapidly beneath the arched roof, flying from one window to another and filling the building with their cries.

The old man explained one or two points of interest to Dalvy's two rustic assistants. In his shirt sleeves and wide woollen trousers, buckled tight with a leather belt, and his bald head ringed at the back by a few curls of white hair and his calm face encircled by a short white beard, the little man resembled an elderly apostle from a painting by Rubens.

Ghisparru, for his part, returning to stand before the altar, found that the small figure of Saint John also resembled someone.

'Hey, Bellia,' he said, nudging his companion, 'who does that saint remind you of?'

The other man looked up and eyed the statue carefully.

'A little black lamb…'

'No, look! A Christian!'

'I don't know.'

'It looks like Giame,' Ghisparru murmured, in respectful tones.

'Who's Giame?' the warden asked, looking up too.

And Bellia stared at the saint again and said: 'The boss's son. This fellow's wife was his wet-nurse and now he takes himself for a kind of foster-father. Anything nice he sees, he thinks it looks like this son. Just wait, my friend, when he gets back from his studies he'll plant his foot… in your behind, and he'll kick you out. Ha, ha!'

Ghisparru did not reply. He turned away to kneel, said a short prayer and then went outside.

Back in the first courtyard, the two servants asked the warden who had founded the church, whether it was a very wealthy one, and how much they paid him.

The old man told them a long story. There was a lady whose body had been invaded by demons and she went about on horseback, by night, riding through the countryside like a spectre. And this lady, *donna* Rofoela Perella, was very devout and always went to church, but when the moment came for the blessing she had to go outside because otherwise she started raving and shouting and hit out at people with the ferocity of a lion. She actually went as far as making a trip to Rome, but not even the Pope had been able to drive the demons out. So then she had made a vow, which was to build and endow a church if she was cured. And one night, as she was out riding, all at once the evil spirits had left her. She got down off her horse, threw herself to the ground, kissed the stones, and promised to build a church on the site, dedicated to Saint John because she was especially devoted to him.

The church now owned lands, money, flocks of animals and received revenue from rents. Many offerings and donations came in also, for the saint. In addition, every year, the warden set out with a horse loaded up with several baskets, while in his arms he carried a small statue of the saint enclosed in a wooden casket with glass sides. And he went from village to village, begging alms for the holy saint.

The pious women of the Nuoro district gave money, wax, wool, grain. In the Barbagia, the baskets were piled high with walnuts, beans and chestnuts. In other places the devout offered cheeses, oil, honey, cattle. All these goods were sold, and in this way the wealth of the saint increased every year, along with his lands and his flocks.

The two servants listened open-mouthed, especially Ghisparru.

'What about you? What do they give you?'

'Give me? Nothing,' the warden said. 'I live on the charity of the pilgrims and devout folk, if they choose to give me anything.'

The two looked at each other: then each took out a small coin and passed it over to him.

'One for me, one for the saint,' said the old man, kissing the coins.

'What's your name? Don't you have any sons?'

'A man who doesn't have a wife doesn't have sons. My name is John Baptist' — he crossed himself — 'son of God and of Saint Anthony. And who are you? Where are you going?'

'We are the assistants of Antonio Dalvy of D...' Bellia said, with a touch of haughty swagger. 'We are travelling in search of foals and mares, which our master buys.'

The little old man looked up.

'Oh? I have a mare! Do you want to buy it?'

'How did you come to have that?'

'How did I come to have it? The way you come to have anything in this world.'

'It couldn't be... plucked?' said Bellia, fluttering the fingers of his right hand then bunching them in. He laughed.

'You can stop your sly laughing,' the old man cried indignantly. 'I was given that mare. A very rich man came to the festival last year. He was as tall as anything, as tall as you and me standing on top of each other. He had a long beard just like an armful of sunbeams bundled together, and his eyes were as blue as the sky. He was a Sardinian gentleman but he lives on the mainland, so out of the kingdom (perhaps he was the Marquis of Morès*). Anyway, he had a high old time and nothing escaped his eye. He was dancing and drinking and all the rest! Anyway, he had this mare, you'll see it, and he raced against the other horses and he won the prize. Anyway, he came up to me and he said something in a language I couldn't understand. I bowed and saluted. Then he said something else. "What are you saying, my lord?" And someone explained: "He's asking you what you do all year." "Ah, my lord, I make mats, baskets, cane stools." "Show me." I show him a mat. "Beautiful, beautiful!" "Well," I say, "if it's beautiful, you can have it as a present." You should have seen his eyes glitter! He says: "Do you like the look of my horse?" I say: "What?" "Do you like the look of my horse?" he says, and points his finger towards the mare. "Very much!" I say. "Well then, it's yours. Grab its bridle, it's yours."'

'You've got the luck of the devil!' Bellia exclaimed. 'And you took it?'

'Of course! I said no at first, but the gentleman was so insistent that in the end I took it. She's a beautiful animal, you should see her! She's black really, but with white flecks all over: you'd think it had snowed on her. Anyway, listen to what happened next. There was a man, a rich farmer, he had people working under him, you know the kind of thing. What does he do, the cunning fox? He thinks: "If he gives that poor devil a mare for making him a present of a rush mat, what will he give me if I give him a really big present?" So immediately he catches his horse by its bridle, it was a bay with white socks, a very pretty animal as well, and he goes up to the gentleman and he says: "Now you have no way of getting home. Take this horse, take it as a present." The gentleman looks him up and down, then he starts to laugh, and what does he do? He accepts the horse and he says: "I'll keep this one for myself." Then I heard that when he got back to his home on the mainland, he sent the farmer a tin of sweetmeats.'

'Very good!' said the servants, who were enjoying the old man's stories. And Bellia added: 'A blow for justice. That gentleman was an eagle in comparison with the farmer.'

'And this mare, can we see it? It's probable the master will buy it, especially now we've almost finished our tour.'

'The mare isn't here. But tomorrow, if you want, I can fetch her here, and meanwhile you can go off and come back with the master.'

So it was agreed. The two servants went off to the neighbouring village and informed their master. And the next day everyone was gathered again at the outer courtyard gateway of the little church.

Bellia took his boss's umbrella, Ghisparru held his horse steady, and Antonio Dalvy dismounted heavily, puffing and opening his green eyes.

Old *Zio* Juanne Battista** went to catch the mare, which was browsing amongst the flowering scrub.

When still a little way off, he threw the slip-knot of a horsehair rope over the animal's neck and led it somewhat reluctantly to stand in front of the merchant.

In truth it was not a very large creature, but once Dalvy had swiftly opened its mouth and felt its back, he realised it was quite a young mare, put to very little work, and decided to acquire it.

'Try her out,' he said to Bellia.

The servant jumped on her, bareback, in a single leap, and dug his heels in her flanks. The animal shot off like an arrow, and to pull her in the servant had to throw himself backwards, tugging hard on the rope.

When they arrived at the bottom of the track, he forced it, with some difficulty, to turn round, and came back panting and calling out: 'My God, it's more like an unbroken foal than a mare. The devil can ride this one.'

'Fine, fine,' Dalvy said, smacking the horse's rump and making the creature shudder. 'It hasn't been broken in properly yet, even though it's not all that young. It's not a very big thing, too short, it looks more like a mule. But as we're here…! Right, how much do you want for it?'

The little old man had been giving the matter much consideration. He had sought advice in fact. Now, however, he found himself somewhat embarrassed by the presence of this substantial person with the eyes of a cat and by his disdainful remarks.

Nevertheless, he recovered a little of his shrewdness and said, as if making a significant concession: 'If it wasn't for the fact that I'm in some need, I wouldn't sell her… Ah, need: your lordship knows our Sardinian proverb, necessity sets even old men running. Anyway, enough… Since it's for you… fifty *scudi*.'***

Dalvy started to laugh. The servants, seeing him laugh, laughed too.

'Goodness me, you're a clever little fellow, my good

72

man! But at the same time it's clear you've never sold horses before.'

'Excuse me, my lord, but…'

'Tell me, what's your name?'

'John Baptist…'

'Well, go and get yourself blessed, *Zio* John Baptist. Are you trying to make me laugh?'

'No, but after all,' the old man said, reddening, 'I've had the mare valued, by someone who knows the business.'

'Are you telling me that I don't know the business?'

'I'm not saying that. All right, what does your lordship say?'

'Look,' Dalvy said, turning towards his own handsome horse. 'You see that one? Well, that one, that one standing there, cost sixty *scudi*.'

'When it was a foal,' Bellia murmured to Ghisparru.

'Shut up, you.'

'You shut up. Silent as a stone. Or else.'

'Go on then, your lordship,' said the warden, cocking an ear in their direction, 'you tell me.'

He was very keen to get rid of the mare, and ended up settling for a hundred and seventy-five lire, which Dalvy paid in brand-new twenty-five lire notes.

'Ah, these are nice,' *Zio* Juanne said, putting them inside a leather wallet. 'If…'

He seemed to want to say something more, but in the presence of the servants didn't dare.

'If your lordship would like to see inside the church?'

'Very well, we'll see the church,' Dalvy answered with condescension.

The servants remained outside.

'Hurry up, *Zio* Juanne,' Ghisparru shouted.

'Ah, it's too much! He calls me *Zio*! He's older than I am!' the warden muttered.

'Ah, but he's a good servant! Not like his companion!' Dalvy confided.

The old man led the merchant into the church, offered him the holy water and showed him everything there was to see.

'Pah!' Dalvy said, puffing out his cheeks good-naturedly. 'Very nice, very nice! Yes, beautiful! It doesn't seem possible, looking from the outside, that it should be so fine inside. And when is the feast day?'

'Thirtieth of May. Quite soon.'

'Pah, pah! Very fine! I'll tell my wife she should come! And bring all her relations with her!' he added, as if to himself, with a smile. 'And her son too, in the holidays. He's a devout one is that boy, like all the rest of them on his mother's side!'

After the church, the warden showed him the *cambussia* used by the priors, then the one used by the chaplain, and several more. When they were outside, he turned somewhat timidly to Dalvy and said: 'If your lordship will permit, I'd like to ask you a favour.'

The other man opened his eyes a little wider and sent the warden a doubtful look.

'I'm not asking for a donation,' the warden said with dignity. 'If you want to give me something, that's your own sense of duty. But that's not it. This is the thing, listen: I've put aside a little money for when I'm thrown on the scrap heap, but it's all in small notes and a bit grubby. What I'm wondering is if you can change them for me.'

In saying this, admitting his great secret, *Zio* Juanne Battista blushed. A little flame flickered rapidly, too, across the features of the merchant.

'Well, if that's all it is!'

'That's all, that's all, nothing else!'

'Bring it to me, bring it to me!'

The old man went into one of the *cumbissias* and came out in a moment with a bundle in his hands. He saw Bellia's head peering round the main gateway, as if spying on them, and he concealed the bundle.

'Your servants are spying on us,' he said quietly. 'It's better they don't see, your lordship will understand.'

'Yes, yes,' the other man agreed, and *Zio* Juanne Battista drew him into the *cumbissia* which was cluttered with newly made mats and baskets. They crossed to the little window, and there, on the ledge of beaten earth, against a fresh background of spring heathland, they exchanged the money.

Antonio Dalvy emerged all red and puffing. He too saw the sallow face and bleary eyes of Bellia peeping round the arch of the central gateway. He crossed the courtyard with rapid strides.

'The stupid fellow, making me waste so much time showing me his little holes in the wall,' he said.

In a minute, while he was remounting his horse with his servants' assistance, *Zio* Juanne Battista reappeared from one of them. He was all cheerful, tightening his belt and rubbing his hands.

'Right, then, goodbye,' the merchant said, settling into the saddle.

'May God and Saint John go with you. And make sure

your wife and son come to the festival, your lordship.'

'Fine, fine,' Dalvy kept repeating, still adjusting himself in the saddle.

His assistants were gathered round him dutifully, tightening the stirrups, adjusting the spurs, no longer paying any attention to the old man.

Eventually everyone was ready. Antonio Dalvy moved off first, with his green umbrella opened. Then the two servants set out, on foot, leading behind them the black mare with its white spots. The poor beast resisted at first, tossing its head back, flicking its tail: it seemed to sense the ending of its liberty.

And *Zio* John Baptist remained alone, in the shade of the gateway, before a great green landscape that stretched around him, all in flower and quite deserted.

Some time afterwards, Bellia, Antonio Dalvy's servant, was arrested, caught in the act of circulating false banknotes. When he was searched, a not inconsiderable sum in notes was found on him, some of them good, the majority forged.

He appeared astonished, or skilfully feigned it. He said the sum of money was his, that they were his savings, the work of ten years. Then he claimed he had found a bundle containing the money and believing it genuine had appropriated it. And in the end he muddled and contradicted himself in a thousand different ways. He was condemned to three years and five months in prison.

He was a man of irascible temperament, cunning and rascally. His sallow face, with its large cleft nose in the middle and two red and bleary eyes, inspired repugnance in any onlooker.

While he was held on remand and the trial was being prepared, he managed to send a trusted messenger to Antonio

Dalvy, telling him to exert every effort to save him, otherwise the merchant would come to regret it sorely.

When questioned, Dalvy had made a favourable statement in defence of his servant, but now, in the face of this threatening demand, he turned red with anger, puffed out his cheeks and only just restrained himself from giving the messenger a good kicking.

'The thieving goat!' he exclaimed. 'What has this got to do with me? I suppose he's going to say I gave him the false notes. Get out of here, and tell him if he utters my name he's going to be His Majesty's guest for a very long time.'

The trusted messenger went away. A few days later he returned and had another discussion with Antonio Dalvy. This time the merchant did not shout. He simply showed the trusted messenger a document in which Bellia undertook to serve *signor* Antonio Dalvy for one whole year without pay after stealing from him one of his fattened oxen.

The theft having been exposed, this was the arrangement they had come to.

'So you can tell him not to bother me again. Go away!'

And he sent the trusted messenger packing for a second time. The man, however, returned for a third time: 'He requests that your lordship at least finds him a good lawyer and pays the fees. And he asks you to send him something to make life easier while he's in prison. And when he comes out, to take him back into service with you.'

'Send him something? A bullet in the guts is what he deserves!' Dalvy shouted, eyes flashing like emeralds. 'As for service, we'll see about that when he's out, which won't be today or tomorrow either. As for the rest, get out from under my feet unless you want a dose of the same yourself.'

The trusted messenger departed, very subdued, and did not return again. Bellia was convicted.

His companions in disgrace witnessed his descent into despair. He gnawed his fists, pulled out his hair, ground his teeth. Even in his sleep he beat his head on his pallet and groaned like a maddened dog.

Then he was taken off to prison far away, and for a long time nothing more was heard of him.

Zio John Baptist continued to weave his mats and baskets in the shade of the gateway, before a great green landscape that stretched around him, all in flower and quite deserted.

Nearly four years had gone by since he had sold the mare to that stout gentleman with the cat's eyes, as he called him, and since he had changed the money.

Only four years: but the warden seemed to have aged ten or twelve. He was sad, gloomy; he looked like a decrepit hermit, overcome by bitter remorse.

In addition, times turned bad: people passed straight by the church, crossing themselves but not stopping, failing even to venture into the outer courtyard. The flow of small coins dried up.

Zio Juanne waited for the festival that year with a certain amount of anxiety. Spring was dying in a splendour of golden corn, of flowering grasses, of burning skies.

From his gateway the old man could see great swathes of poppies blazing like live coals, and further on, towards the horizon, meadowlands entirely covered in violet flowers.

Nothing stirred in that magnificent solitude; only, at night, under the clear stars, the warm breath of wild scents, joined in the distance by the slow clinking of sheep bells, peaceful and melancholy.

But with the onset of darkness, *Zio* Juanne became even more sad and gloomy. He would walk round the courtyards, trembling; often he would fall to the ground and pray, fearing that one day they would find him there dead, half eaten by the ravens.

Towards the middle of May, the prior appeared. He was a local man, wealthy, with a red waistcoat and a white beard. He inspected everything, had the chaplain's rooms swept and scrubbed, and departed. A few days later he returned at the head of a long train of people from the surrounding countryside, all mounted on horses.

The prior was holding a banner of green brocade with long streamers. Then came the chaplain in a black frock-coat, then other local men all dressed in red, on their little horses with their women seated up behind, and children in scarlet caps, their foreheads covered by broad bands of black silk; and weary dogs, panting, tongues hanging out.

When they were still some way off, the men began to discharge their guns and hurl into the air great shouts of joy.

Zio Juanne pulled on the bell rope and the bell rang, and its note, thin and cracked, rose and was lost in the blue of the sky.

The people arrived, dismounted, entered the church; and the women brought offerings of wax, of coins, of lace, of embroidery, of flowers.

Then each family selected a *cumbissia*: the men fetched armfuls of grass and scented branches and scattered them in a corner of the little rooms; the women spread them out, laid

79

mattresses over them, blankets, prepared the pallets, knocked nails into the walls, hung on them the utensils brought from home.

Then they swept the church and the courtyards, and the men cleaned the well, whose water, like everything else to do with the church, had miraculous properties according to the local populace.

The two courtyards were turned into a little village. The little church bell kept ringing, swung on by small boys who were already violent and rough and who raced through the surrounding fields, bringing the vast solitude to life with their incessant comings and goings and their wild birds' shrill cries.

The chaplain was still standing at the altar, legs straddled, the tassel of his skull-cap falling over one ear. A sea of pilgrims was gathered round him, with faces of every type, like figures in a painting. And everyone was shouting and laughing.

The women attended to their domestic matters inside the little rooms. Meanwhile the prioress and the women of the festival committee had other duties. (They owed their position to ancient rights of heredity, as descendants of the church's founders. The prioresses were elected, turn by turn, from within their number.) Every day they cooked great pans of soup and country-style macaroni, or a mash of wheat-grain with fresh cheese; and they distributed this to their families and to a horde of poor people, ill-smelling beggars who had come to hover in the outer courtyard, their sole and sorry aim to obtain a share of this food, be it soup or lowly wheat-grain.

The church, newly cleaned and made fragrant, and enlivened by the trilling and darting flights of the swallows, was quickly invaded and profaned by these beggars, who tainted the air, scratched themselves, and refused to make room, even when asked, for civilised people. And they constantly quarrelled with each other, itched, scratched and begged at every hour of the day or night.

There was no lack of devout and cleanly-washed pilgrims either. They came on foot, shoeless, bare-headed; indeed, some women even wore their hair loose. They crawled on their knees from the door to the altar, sometimes even from the outer gateway, and brought offerings of money, of wax, of jewels, tresses of hair. If they paid a certain amount, the chaplain put on his surplice, bent his head to put on his stole, the prior took up his green banner, and a procession wound through the inner courtyard round the church. If they paid double, the procession wound through both courtyards.

Then the pilgrim would cleanse himself religiously in the water at the well; afterwards the prior would catch the pilgrim's arm, take him over to the women, who served him with wine, coffee, honeyed sweetmeats and fixed him with intense stares while asking where he came from.

The prior ended up as drunk as a brute beast.

If a married couple arrived, the woman was required to kiss the serving ladle to guarantee her becoming a good housewife; the husband drew a measure of water from the well to make him, in his life, a good worker.

And all the pilgrims were required, out of devotion, at least to have a taste of either the soup or the wheat-grain.

In the mornings the chaplain said mass, in the evenings the novena. No one was allowed to miss these services. At the end of the novena, whilst the countryside beyond slipped slowly towards sleep and a pink dusk descended on the bright circle of the horizon, the people gathered in the church sang the '*gosos*' — praises to the saint — in an antique form of Spanish. And that rhythmical dirge, with its melancholy tune, at that hour of roseate shadows, lost in the vastness of that lonely landscape, resounded more than ever with the nostalgic chants of old Sardinia. It was like an ancient people, still semi-barbarous, waking up, as it were, after long centuries of slumber, into the present age.

At night, flames leapt from campfires. Lentisk wood crackled, juniper scented the air. The priors extemporised chants in vainglorious competition; the eyes of the women grew languid with reverie.

And *Zio* John Baptist?

Zio John Baptist was rarely to be seen. He attended mass, then, hovering close by the door, received the small coin that was the pilgrims' offering. At midday he went to the prioress with a bowl which was filled with steaming soup or spelt. Then he disappeared. Sometimes he could be heard shouting at the beggars who were despoiling the church.

'Take yourself off, you wretch.'

'I'm not going anywhere.'

'If you don't shift I'll shift you with a big stick.'

'And the devil will take a stick to you.'

'Scabby wretch.'

'Bald old fool.'

'Filth!'

'What's wrong with you?' the prior asked. 'You're more bad-tempered this year than you were last.'

'It's death coming closer.'

'Well, let it come. We'll box its ears.'

82

'Ah, it's no laughing matter!'

Meanwhile the saint's feast day drew nearer. On the eve, people arrived in great numbers. Groups of men and women appeared from every village and every group carried aloft its own banner.

As soon as they slid from the saddle they entered the church, and as soon as they were out of it they set to dancing their Sardinian dances. And the people of one village ridiculed and laughed at the others' dances. There wasn't a person, from this group or that, who didn't find something to mock.

And everybody was laughing.

Pedlars, purveyors of wines and spirits, dealers in spurs and bridles set up shop in some of the smaller stalls in the outer courtyard. The crowds, consequently, were thick there, while the inner courtyard remained practically deserted.

The wildest of the groups was a troop of swarthy peasants, drunk and red-faced, who sang and danced to the rhythms of their own strange poetry.

> *'Assa festa 'e Gasta so andadu,*
> *'La chi enit in primu eranu:*
> *'Inie b'er Baròre — b'er Baròre,*
> *'Inie b'er Baròre e Bastianu,*
> *'In Paghe e cuncordia buffende:*
> *'E da chi la idèi — la idèi,*
> *'E da chi la idèi fugudende,*
> *'Rughei unu mortu, unu latadu,*
> *'Assa gesta 'e Gasta so andadu.'*

'To the feast of Gasta went I,
'In the springtime of the year:
'The Saviour is here — the Saviour's here,
'The Saviour and Sebastian,
'In peace and harmony drinking.
'And the moment I saw it — saw it,
'And the moment I saw it, at once
'I fell, a dead man, a wounded.
'To the feast of Gasta went I.'

They put a particular stress on the lines:

'Inie b'er Baròre — b'er Baròre'

and

'E da chi la idèi — la idèi'

repeating them over and over, with modulations, turning them into the rhythm that animated the dance.

However, they sang new lines whenever they saw people from a different village approach.

A priest arrived on horseback, for instance, wearing a frock coat and short britches and clutching a wide umbrella against the pommel of the saddle. He looked like a figure from a magic lantern show.

Someone said: 'He's from Nuoro.'

And immediately the dancing group broke into a new quatrain:

'In Santu Predu han pesadu unu ballu,
'A sonos de ghitarra e fiolinu;
'Sos prideros non jughen collarinu,
'Ca lis ha fattu in trughu unu callu.
'In Santu Predu han pesadu unu ballu.'

'In San Pietro' (near Nuoro) 'what a dance I saw,
'To the sounds of guitars and violins;
'The priests were collarless under their chins,
'For their collars rubbed their necks red raw.
'In San Pietro what a dance I saw.'

And the crowd laughed. Wild cries rang out, carrying like a horse's whinnying above the constant hubbub of the dancing songs.

The beggars planted themselves at the side of the track, a certain distance apart, their hands held out, intoning a ceaseless litany of lamentations.

Late on in the evening of the vigil, *Zio* Juanne Battista chanced to find himself near one of these beggars when he saw a woman and a young man arrive, followed by a peasant who looked like a servant.

The woman must have been a lady from the villages around: she was stout, with sagging cheeks. Her choice of clothes showed signs of affectation: a black corseted waistcoat, tightly fastened, decorated with jet trimmings, a wide skirt of yellow material. Over her head she had spread a large scarf in violet damask; and, even though no longer young, she was adorned with strings of coral necklace. She was riding a docile black mare with spotted white markings.

85

The young man must have been quite tall, for his back curved forwards in the saddle. He had the face of a pale child and from his cap, pushed to the back of his head, sprang a tuft of ginger hair.

As soon as the beggars saw these lordly-looking people coming they began to repeat their lamentations with double the force. The voice of one of them rose high above the others, and all of them shrilled like so many crickets.

'Giame,' said the woman in mournful tones, 'do something for these poor wretches.'

The young man slowed his horse's pace and, with two fingers, began to extract from his waistcoat pocket small coins of copper and silver.

'For you. Take it.'

'For you.'

'You too. Here.'

His grace and goodness towards those poor people were exceptional; they, for their part, never ceased asking, nor blessing him for what they received.

He brought his horse to a halt, bent low, and laid pieces of small change on the open and filthy palms of the beggars.

The woman walked the mare slowly forwards. The servant followed, closely watching the young man's every move.

Coming up to *Zio* Juanne Battista, Giame dropped a coin into the pouch of the beggar who was, or was pretending to be blind. Then he dug out another coin and passed it to the elderly warden.

The latter, who was staring at the newcomers wide-eyed, proudly pushed the gift of alms aside.

'I am no beggar.'

'Forgive me, then,' the young man said humbly.

Zio Juanne Battista was moved; he detained the kindly young gentleman for a moment to say: 'I am the warden of this church, and I know that mare.' He pointed a finger towards the animal. 'That mare was once mine.'

'Oh! It was yours?'

'Yes, mine, I say so as a true Christian!' the old man exclaimed, putting a hand to his heart.

Meanwhile, as the blind man was feeling in his pouch for the coin and blessing in a sing-song voice the person who had given it, the servant caught up with them.

'Greetings, *Zio* John Baptist,' he called, bringing his mount to a halt.

The old man looked at that large unkempt head with its long and shaggy grey hair, and quickly recognised the servant. He returned the greeting, then addressed himself again to the young man.

'Is your lordship perhaps the son of the gentleman I sold the mare to four years ago? The creature is steadier now, obviously, but I recognised her straightaway. And then I recognise this man too. Your lordship's father was a well-built man, with the eyes of a cat.'

'Just so!' Giame said, laughing.

'Oh, your lordship has greenish eyes as well! It's clear you're his son!' the little old man exclaimed, fixing his eyes on Giame. 'Well anyway, if you two need anything — the lady there is your mother, is that not so? — you have only to ask.'

'We need accommodation for the night,' Ghisparru said.

'Good, fine, come with me, let me show you the way,

we'll arrange everything.'

The warden moved off, walking at the side of the young man's horse.

When they reached the outer gateway, where *donna* Lillica was waiting, the young man swung his horse round, pulled his cap down over his brow and stared out at the landscape.

The sun had disappeared, but the whole plain around them, all the luxuriant, golden green vegetation, the fiery poppies, the silvery lines of corn, the meadows thick with violet flowers, and finally every bushy thicket, every stalk and stem, seemed to stand, motionless and glowing, as if joining in some mystical contemplation of the sunset.

The fading sky was pure, a nacreous blue with no gradations, even towards the west where the sun had disappeared like a pearl.

Giame felt a rush of joy at the sight of such beauty. And not even the presence and the voices of the beggars camped along the track, not even the shouting and barbarous singing of the crowds, profaning the solemnity of the hour and the countryside, could diminish the light in his heart.

He smiled, with those fine gleaming eyes. He would have liked to kneel, to salute the beautiful evening, the beautiful countryside. He would have like to hurl into the air a shout of joy.

They crossed the outer courtyard.

The men from the various districts were still dancing, holding their women, wearily smiling, by the hand.

'E da chi la idèi — la idèi,
'E da chi la idèi — la idèi,
'E da chi la idèi — la idèi...'

88

And quite a large group was gathered round a man dressed in moleskin with a blue silk scarf round his neck. He was telling some kind of story, and everyone was laughing and interrupting his tale with salty remarks.

Seeing Giame and his mother pass by, a rustic fellow shouted: '*Bibat sa dama!* (Long live the lady!)'

'*E su cavaglieri!* (And her handsome knight!),' some of the others responded.

The small crowd of listeners turned round with a laugh. The man with the blue scarf stood up, stared, then sat down again and resumed his story.

The dancers sang, in honour of lady Lillica:

> '*Ca er bessida missignora,*
> '*S'alligret d'ogni mutagna:*
> '*Paret s'istella aurora, etc.'*

> 'The mountains all with joy do shout,
> 'Because my lady has come out:
> 'See how the morning star she flouts, etc.'

In the meantime Giame, his mother and the servant dismounted outside the warden's little chamber.

Donna Lillica shook out her clothes and took a few steps up and down, her limbs numb from the journey.

'This man,' Giame told her, introducing the old man, 'is the warden of the church. He recognised the mare. He's the one who sold her, to Papa.'

'True. He did,' Ghisparru said.

89

'Yes, by my faith, I did sell her, for thirty-five *scudi*,' the old man echoed, stroking the animal. 'Do you remember, eh, little dove? You're still the same; a bit better behaved though. You've been eating barley and straw, eh! Your coat's like a mirror. Well, anyway, your lord- and ladyship can install yourselves here, in my little room. There are mats here already, and then we'll ask the prior for some blankets.'

While Ghisparru, helped by Giame, unloaded the bags and lifted the saddles from the horses, *donna* Lillica continued to stretch her legs by walking up and down, and adjusted her scarf and necklace. She wished to enter the church with due decorum.

A number of ladies presented themselves at the church doors. They looked at her with curiosity, greeted her with smiles, sensing her to be a lady of wealth.

At that moment the man in moleskin with the blue scarf round his neck entered the courtyard. He approached, spreading his arms wide and shouting:

'Greetings, *donna* Lillica! Greetings, my lady! Greetings!'

'Bellia, is that really you? Here?'

It was the former servant, recently returned from prison.

'I'm really here! Or doesn't it look like it, my lady? I've come to intercede with Saint John the Baptist to touch the heart of Antonio Dalvy and make him give me my job back. Ha, ha!'

He laughed loudly, a malicious laugh. Giame and the warden were inside the little room. Ghisparru was holding the horses' bridles, and when he saw Bellia and saw too that he was drunk, he looked at him with contempt.

'Hey!' he called. 'This is no place to try to do business. You have come alone, we have come alone: so there's no one to do your business with.'

Bellia was initially startled, then he laughed again, staring at the servant.

'Aha! Are you here too, so-called foster-father? Good, in that case we'll talk business with you, and with the lady and with that wet-nursed boy…'

'Go away, you need to lie down!' Ghisparru shouted, moving towards him.

'And with him as well!' Bellia shouted in turn, pointing to *Zio* Juanne, who was emerging with Giame.

The old man looked at him in confusion, failing to recognise him in the clothes he was wearing. But he too realised the man was drunk.

'Don't you recognise me, *Zio* John Baptist, son of Saint Anthony?'

'We are all sons of God!' the old man replied, offended. 'And whose son are you? And who knows it?'

'Who knows it? I know it! But you don't know. You're the son of Saint Anthony: and I'm the son of the things I've done in life.'

'Fine things they were, too!' said *donna* Lillica, walking away in the direction of the church.

Bellia turned, followed her with his eyes, laughed again.

'Say your prayers well, my lady. Pray for them all, men and cattle, lizards and foxes, vultures and doves…'

'And asses! Go away, go on, go and lie down!' Ghisparru told him threateningly.

'Yes, I'm going away to lie down, because I've drunk too much. But it's not just wine I've got inside me; it's other things as well, it's bile, it's wormwood, it's poison, it's knives.

I'm going, I'm going, no need to get angry, little doctor. But tomorrow, when I'm sober, we'll have a talk together. And with that one too!'

The drunkard turned to the warden again, fixing him with his bleary but burning little eyes.

Zio Juanne stared back; and it seemed to him that he had seen him before, and a vague memory, slightly worrying, fluttered in his mind without his being able to grasp it.

And he too said:

'Go away, go away and lie down.'

In the meantime, along with Ghisparru and Giame, he bustled about, settling the horses in an empty stall, strapping nosebags to their necks and directing their heads into the little sacks filled with straw. Bellia watched, swaying on his legs, the air around him stinking of liquor.

'You don't recognise me,' he said to the old man. 'Well, I'll tell you who I am. I'm Bellia Fava, servant of Antonio Dalvy, the man who bought the mare which some mad gentleman from the mainland gave you as a present.'

The old man's eyes widened, he made a strange gesture; but he quickly recovered and said:

'If anyone's mad, it's you, you snake, not that gentleman. Go, go. Go away and lie down.'

'Go, go,' Giame joined in, bending down and brushing straw off the hems of his trousers.

By sheer dint of repetition the idea of going away and lying down seemed to penetrate the drunkard's brain.

'Yes, yes, I'm going. I'm going to lie down under a bush. Yes, I'll go all right, and I'll vomit up all the wine and hard liquor inside me. But there are other things I need to get out of me as well. Fine, we'll speak again; I'll come and find you tonight.'

And he went away.

'Go to the devil!' Ghisparru said.

'Quiet! Don't provoke him,' Giame muttered. Then turning to the warden, he asked: 'Now then, in a couple of words, tell me about the lady who founded this church. She was said to be possessed by demons.'

Zio Juanne happily repeated the story of *donna* Rofoela Peralla.

Giame listened closely, his shoulders leaning against the wall; and the servant also listened, but with an air of anxiety and irritation.

Having heard the legend, they made their way into the church. The servant folded his cap and placed it on a step and knelt on it.

His rugged face rose towards the little figure of the saint dressed in skins, and his lips moved in fervent prayer.

In the middle of the church, on a piece of yellow material, stood the wood and glass casket used for carrying the saint round the villages in quest of alms. Two candles drew sparkling reflections from the glass, behind which the statue held out its little arms. A white lamb nibbled at the saint's short tunic.

Before leaving the church, the devout knelt on the edge of the coarse yellow carpet, prayed, kissed the casket and left their offerings on a metal tray.

Giame observed all this, circling the yellow carpet on tip-toe, then began to decipher the memorial tablets. The rosy glow of dusk died slowly in the roof vault of the little church; a few swallows still swooped, their cries only faint.

Giame was searching the memorial tablets for the legend of the lady who, possessed, rode out by night over that wild landscape, one dying spring long years ago. But very soon he received a shock, finding on one tablet that the founders of the church had been seven in number. Amongst them was the famous *donna* Raffaella Perella De-Castra, but there was no mention of nocturnal horse rides, of demons, of journeys to Rome.

'Perhaps there are other documents, though.' Giame thought. And he turned round. He saw his mother and Ghisparru kneeling on the yellow carpet, with which *donna* Lillica's luxuriant yellow skirt made a matching splash of colour. But Giame's attention was fully drawn to the demeanour of the servant, who was praying with feverish intensity. 'What kind of prayer can that be?' he thought.

And he stood watching him closely. From the windows there drifted in on the breeze a cool scent of grasses, and from the courtyards still came the chorus of the rustics' songs.

> *'Inie b'er Baròre — b'er Baròre,*
> *'Inie b'er Baròre — b'er Baròre,*
> *'Inie b'er Baròre — b'er Baròre,*
> *'Inie b'er Baròre — e Bustianu.'*

Meanwhile *Zio* Juanne Battista was looking for the prior to alert him to the arrival of a rich lady and her grown-up son and urge him to find them and present his compliments.

Passing into the outer courtyard he saw that Bellia, instead of finding somewhere to lie down, had seated himself once more on the side wall of one of the stalls, among a group of drunken men, and was regaling them, half in Sardinian, half in Italian, with unsavoury stories about his prison companions.

The old man stopped for a moment, staring again at Bellia's bleary eyes and bright blue scarf.

As soon as he spotted the warden he stood up, calling out:

'Hey there, son of Saint Anthony.'

And he sat down again, laughing.

Zio Juanne started, and immediately remembered something terrible.

As soon as the prior, a man of quality too in his own esteem, had received the warden's message, he went to the Dalvys, showered them with compliments and led them to his own quarters. There, he introduced them to his wife, a large and stately peasant woman wearing several strings of necklaces and medallions.

'Grascia, this is a lady, and this is a man of learning. Quick, bring coffee, bring cordials, bring sweetmeats, chestnuts, everything you have… in our modest way, *signori*,' he added, bowing slightly, like a gentleman.

But the wife was unruffled, rather haughty even. She seemed not at all confused, indeed, it was as if she was making a great concession by complimenting the visitors. She gave *donna* Lillica the most comfortable seat in the *cumbissia*, noted her necklace and said with dignity:

'Here we live out in the country. We do what we can.'

Meanwhile the serving women prepared the coffee. In a corner of the room a pretty little girl in a red cap, her forehead fringed with a thick band of black silk, was rocking a baby boy who was making the cheeping sounds of a young bird and waving his little arms in the air.

'Peep-peep, little lamb!' the women were saying, turning round to the infant every now and then.

'Hurry up, ladies, hurry up!' the prior called, pouring a green liquor into goblets. 'This is a lady, this is a man of learning.'

And he snatched the cover from the basket of sweetmeats, throwing them all into a jumble. He was red in the face, his beard was rumpled, his jacket unfastened.

His wife was secretly angry, but to keep her composure she ignored him, not even looking at him, apparently fully intent on paying compliments to the lady.

Giame observed all these things.

The prior invited them to the dinner which was to be given by the chaplain and would admit neither demurral nor thanks. He said:

'We need to act like men. We need to eat, drink, accept invitations. We need to show ourselves people of the world, we need to act like men.'

To show themselves people of the world, the Dalvys were obliged to accept the invitation.

Shortly afterwards, the chaplain arrived in person, and then another two or three farmers from the area. All of them wanted to take the Dalvys off here, there and everywhere, offering them every kindness despite not even knowing their names.

'Very well,' Giame said, escaping the company for a moment. 'I'm just going out and I'll be back straightaway.'

He went to look for the servant. The shades of night were gently falling, the evening sky full of stars, and noises faded in the fragrant air. The crowd had partly broken up as some of its members went off into the bushes and scrub, breaking off branches of lentisk and dragging them away to build the bonfire for Saint John outside the main gate.

'Ghisparru,' Giame said when he found the servant, 'we have been invited to dinner. My mother will be sleeping in the prioress's quarters. You can eat with the warden. Keep an eye on the horses.'

He lingered a moment before the limpid horizon, contemplating the solitary poetry of the heath, unspoiled by the hordes of people.

Behind him, in the courtyards, a certain silence gradually settled. The crowd was eating dinner.

Ghisparru and *Zio* Juanne Battista impaled a whole cheese on a wooden spit and roasted it over a slow fire. Then the servant also took from his master's bag some wine, some bread rolls the colour of ivory, butter and salt. And they ate.

'Does your master have many children?' the warden asked.

'This one, and two daughters married to rich gentlemen.'

'Very rich?'

'Rich as the oceans. Ah, yes, they're rich all right. And the master started out with nothing, you know? He went round the country buying lambs' skins.'

'A man with enough will power,' *Zio* Juanne said sagely, 'can turn lambs' skins into lions' skins. And this son is your foster-child, so to speak?'

'He is my foster-child. He calls me step-father.'

'And he's an educated man?'

'He's been to the university.'

For a while the servant, who seemed preoccupied and sad,

remained silent. Then he stirred himself and began to speak of Giame with enthusiastic affection.

'Yes,' he continued, 'he's been to the university! But don't think that makes him old. He's only twenty-two. I can clearly remember when he was born. My wife was his wet-nurse, so we were often in their house. When he received his degree, last year, the whole district celebrated. Because he writes in the paper. And then he's such a good man! He's as innocent as a lizard. They brought him grain and wine and honey, and oranges and lambs' wool. You'd have thought it was a wedding. And he wouldn't harm a fly. He's still studying, all the time, and he's got a good word for everyone. He goes round all the sheepfolds and gets the shepherds to tell him their stories, and then he writes them down.'

'Ah,' the warden remarked, 'that's why he wanted to know the story of lady Rofoela Perella?'

'Listen, *Zio* Juanne. He fell ill in March. He nearly died. So then I made this vow: Saint John the Baptist, make him well again, and I promise I will bring him to your festival. Then he got better. I told him about it. He used to be a deep believer in God, but not so much now. So he started to laugh. He said: "Where is this church?" So I tell him: "Oh, up on the heath somewhere." And I tell him all about it. The story of *donna* Rofoela intrigued him, and so he said: "All right, we'll go, it must be beautiful up there, and after all, you're my second father." When he heard about it, Antonio Dalvy got as mad as a dog, and cursed me like a devil. Then *donna* Lillica said: "In that case, I'll go as well, instead of you." Antonio Dalvy carried on being furious, but then he left to go on one of his trips, and we've come here.'

'Ah, that lady's strong-minded, eh?'

'And no mistake!' Ghisparru said.

'And she's not short of necklaces!' the warden remarked a touch maliciously.

'She's very keen on her necklaces, and on other things as well!'

Dinner over, the two old men went outside. The courtyards were coming back to life. A column of smoke, an acrid smell of lentisk rose and expanded above the fire beginning to take light on the flat ground.

The Dalvys' horses were jostling into one another, pawing the ground, making a tremendous uproar in their stall.

'It would be a good idea to water them and take them out to feed,' the warden said.

'What if they get stolen?'

'Of course they won't!'

Ghisparru walked across to the stall and tried to calm the animals; but they only became worse, kicking out against the walls and stamping on the ground.

So the servant went to find his master and mistress, who were dining with the chaplain. They had finished eating and the only people still at table were the men and lady Lillica, and the serving women were also there. Nearly all the guests were drunk, their faces flushed, their eyes and teeth very bright.

Giame was asking about the festival, how it came to be founded, its customs, and everyone was answering, for the most part with absurd replies which made him smile.

Seeing Ghisparru, he rose quickly from the table and went over to him.

'What is it?' he asked, wiping his mouth with his napkin.

'The horses are very disturbed, they're jostling and kicking each other. It would be better to untie them and let them out into the meadow.'

'As you like. Perhaps it would be better too, then, if you slept outside to guard them.'

'Yes,' the servant said. And he stood silent for a moment, thinking. Then he added, 'I'll be by that gate at the bottom of the track. In case you need to find me.'

'I can't think why!'

'No, but then, sometimes…!'

He went out, returned to the stall, unfastened the nosebags from the horses' collars and dragged them behind him, reluctant and pawing at the ground, with a savage vigour one would not have thought he possessed.

As he passed the big bonfire of lentisk branches, around which the peasants were dancing and singing like wild things, he looked to check if Bellia was to be seen. He was not there. He had not seen him since dusk.

'He'll be sleeping,' he thought. 'And if he's sleeping, he won't be waking up soon, that's for sure.'

He continued on down the track, followed noisily by the horses, and made his way towards the stream. Once there, he slackened and removed the ropes from the horses' necks, and soon they were dipping their noses in the water beneath the motionless tamarisks.

Down here all was silent. The church was visible, lit up by the bonfire, and the red glow spread across the open land and all the way down the track, where it gleamed on the placid waters, on the motionless tamarisks.

But the sounds did not reach this far, and for a few moments only the gurgles from the throats of the drinking horses broke the silence. After that, nothing. The horses dashed off into the scrubby fields, and Ghisparru stretched out on the grass, but he did not close his eyes. His heart felt heavy; and he waited in anguish.

It might have been about eleven o'clock.

Lady Lillica had retired with the prioress, and *Zio* Juanne Battista had prepared Giame's bed with two mats, and a red cushion and yellow blanket borrowed from the chaplain.

Now the little man was waiting, sitting on the threshold of his room. A cool air filled the deserted courtyard: through the open gateways the dull glow of the bonfire could be seen slowly dying away, and an illuminated section of the heath.

The dances had ended, but a few melancholy songs still rose in the clear night from a handful of groups.

Zio Juanne was feeling cheerful, in a way he had not done for a long time. The wine, the food, all the talking, the idea of sleeping in the near presence of a lady of quality, had left him in a daze.

He felt warm all over, a delicious torpor seeping through him. Even he — the elderly hermit — had succumbed to his own mild intoxication.

Suddenly he saw a man come into the courtyard and approach him. He quickly distinguished the bright blue scarf of Bellia, and started. It was as if the former servant caused him a kind of physical terror.

'What do you want?' he asked.

Bellia sat on the ground close to the doorway. He began to speak, in a hoarse voice, and his breath still smelled of wine, but he seemed less drunk than before.

'What do I want? I'm waiting for the professor, the young master. Can you see him over there, by the bonfire? He's looking quite merry, his pasty face has gone all flushed. Do you see him, *Zio* Juanne Battista?'

'I can't see anything,' the old man said.

'You don't see anything, but I see everything. It's a girl, tall, thin as a stick, with blue eyes and a complexion whiter than her blouse. Can't you see her? Are you blind? The little professor's standing close to her and saying: "Sing me one of your country songs, pretty girl."'

And with his eyes fixed on some distant point, Bellia began to hum the refrain from a song sung in the Logudoro district; then he said: 'He's quite merry, the little professor. Do you think he's drunk as well?'

'What's it to me?'

'Man and wine, they're made for each other. So, then, he's drunk, you're drunk, I'm drunk.'

'You may be. I'm not,' *Zio* Juanne Battista said fiercely.

'I slept in a clump of tamarisk, with my feet in the water. The grasshoppers were jumping all round my head: it made me think of those gaolers again.'

'What gaolers?' the old man asked.

But Bellia made no reply, lost in a sombre vision of his own.

After a short silence, he asked: 'And Ghisparru?'

'I don't know.'

Neither man spoke for a while. Then Bellia burst out, with a tremor in his voice: 'What gaolers? The ones in that place! They were like wild beasts. And then, the hunger! And not a thing ever passing my lips. I don't know how I came out of there alive.'

Zio Juanne understood what he was talking about, and suddenly asked:

'But what do you want from the young master?'

'What do I want from the young master? A business matter!' Bellia replied, sardonically.

'But couldn't you go to where he lives and speak to him there?'

'No, no, it has to be here! — Ah, here they are, they're coming back in.'

'You should go to bed,' said the old man sharply. 'Let people get some rest.'

Bellia turned on him with bitter rage.

'I'll give you rest, you old degenerate! If you don't shut up I'll take you by the scruff of the neck and crush you like a grasshopper. I'm a man! I've been to hell and come out alive! And I know a lot of secrets, you old lizard!'

The old man suddenly felt feeble, abject, and fell silent. The people were coming back inside, the bonfire was no more than embers.

'They've all been drinking too much,' said Bellia with contempt. 'Look how they're walking, weaving about on shaky legs. Ah, the heat from the bonfire has done its work! Even that old crow of a chaplain...! Still, that's what people go to festivals for, to drink... And other things as well!' he concluded.

'*Zio* John Baptist?' Giame called, approaching with the prior.

'I'm here!' the old man answered.

'Who is this man?' the prior asked.

'A man!' Bellia replied.

'Ah, is that you, Bellia?' Giame said.

'It is.'

'Well, good night, and thank you, until tomorrow,' said Giame to the prior.

'Thank *you*, and good night, and until tomorrow. And good night.'

'Good night.'

'And good night,' said Bellia.

The prior departed, humming. Giame asked the warden, playfully:

'And is my bed ready?'

'It's ready, your lordship. But this man…' Bellia, who had leapt to his feet, let him go no further:

'Hey, what are you saying? Leave the talking to me. This man wishes to speak to your lordship.'

'Tomorrow,' Giame said.

'No, now, immediately, and in there…' He pointed a finger towards the church, still open and lit by lanterns.

'Go to bed, Bellia. We'll speak tomorrow.'

The servant raised his voice:

'Don't imagine I'm still drunk, *signor* Giame. The reason I want to speak to you is to tell you something important, something you'll remember all your life.'

Giame was struck by the servant's words and tone. 'Very well,' he said abruptly, shaking his head, 'let's go and hear this something.'

'And you're coming too,' Bellia said, beckoning him forward.

'What's it got to do with me?'

'Come.'

'You come too, then,' Giame said.

Zio Juanne closed the door to his room and followed the other two into the deserted church, lit by lamps hanging high in the roof. The lower parts of the walls and the floor remained in semi-darkness.

The lanterns cast long swaying shadows on the floor; the yellow carpet with the little casket stood in the gloom in the middle of the church. The three men sat down at the back of the church, Bellia in the middle, Giame to his right, *Zio* Juanne to his left.

The warden inclined his head towards the others to hear better. He was acutely curious.

'There's no one here then?' Bellia demanded.

'I think you can see that for yourself! The only ones here are the saints.'

'Right, just what I need: the saints and God can be witnesses that I'm telling the truth.'

'Get on with it, I'm sleepy,' Giamo said curtly.

'Right, professor Giame,' Bellia continued in his hoarse voice. 'Well, I feel fine. So, in a few words. I'm just out of prison, where I went through so much suffering and starvation I'm now ill. I'm a lost man. Antonio Dalvy could and should have saved me, and he didn't. He had no compassion. Then, when I was released, instead of taking me back into his service he drove me away like a mangy dog. Clear off, get out of here, he said, and waved his arms as if he was chasing off some animal.'

'Go on.'

'All right, you can chase the dog away, Antonio Dalvy.

But the dog can bite you.'

'Right! Enough!' Giame exclaimed, rising to his feet. 'What's this thing you have to tell my father? If you don't get to the point, I'm going, animal!'

'Yes, yes, animal. Sit down, little professor, if you please. Just a few more words, which I need to say to this little old man here. You listen.'

'To me?' *Zio* Juanne said.

'To you. You remember, you old weasel, four years ago Ghisparru and I, and our master, Antonio Dalvy, came by here and we bought from you a mare. True, yes or no?'

'Perfectly true.'

'Right, when we bought the mare, Antonio Dalvy paid you in new banknotes. And you said to yourself: these notes are very nice! True, yes or no? Perfectly true. Right, so after that you said to Antonio Dalvy: if your lordship likes, I'll show you the church and the rooms round the courtyard. True? And you took him off with you. Then when you came out you asked if he'd do you the favour of exchanging for new notes a sum of money you had saved in old notes… Don't deny it…'

'But I…'

'But you be quiet, old degenerate! Deny it if you can! Swear before that saint there it isn't true! Swear! Swear that Antonio Dalvy did not go into your *cumbissia* with you and that he did not change your money for you!'

'Well yes, it's true!' *Zio* Juanne Battista admitted. Giame's face turned dark. Something like a vast shadow passed before his eyes. And he listened intently, his entire soul in suspense.

'Now listen, old vulture, while I continue the story. You had a leather pouch with the money in it. You'd hidden it under

106

a stone, which in turn was covered by the earth on the floor. Wait, there's more. One night, a month after we'd taken your mare away, the thirteenth of June, me and Ghisparru Porru, the foster-father of this professor, were travelling in these parts on the master's business. We slept out, up on the heath. And you, old vulture, that night you were sleeping peacefully in your *cumbissia* when you heard a noise. A man had climbed in through the little window and was poking about on the floor where you had hidden your pouch. There was a moon that night, do you remember, old man? In the light of that moon, the man who had climbed through your window saw that you were moving, that your eyes were as wide as saucers. What does he do straightaway? He jumps on you, puts his hands round your neck and squeezes. Then he throws you back against all the mats and baskets, takes the pouch and clears out. Goodbye. He thought he'd killed you, but you're like a cat with nine lives, I wish the devil would strangle you for real. Is it true, all this, or not true?'

'Ah, it was really you!' *Zio* Juanne said, shaking. 'It's true.'

'Right, it was me. I've finished now, *signor* Giame. And I've been in prison because the notes Antonio Dalvy gave this little old man were forged.'

Giame did not answer. He had guessed from the start, and now he heard nothing, saw nothing. The vast shadows enveloped him, suffocated him. A heavy band encircled his head, crushing it.

Bellia looked at him; and for a moment he felt pity for the shrunken face of a terrified youth. What then happened inside that enigmatic but noxious soul? Perhaps the need to console

Giame by showing him that all men are wicked.

'And do you know why this old hermit, this saintly man failed to report what had happened? I'll tell you, little professor. Because the money he'd given to Antonio Dalvy had been stolen from the saint. It was the alms he collected for the saint from the devout, and which this man had put in his own pocket.'

Now *Zio* Juanne was also frozen with terror. How did the man know his guilty secret? Was he the devil? Wide-eyed, he looked at them fearfully in turn, now Giame, now Bellia.

And he would have liked to run from the church and hide himself away; but he could not; and he felt agonisingly rooted to the spot. Giame suddenly demanded: 'And Ghisparru, did he know?'

'Yes, when they arrested me I let him know where I'd been on the night of June thirteenth when I'd left him sleeping on the heath. But not even he was prepared to say a good word for me… and… he knew the whole story, the old goat…and…'

Giame let him go no further.

'Get out, get out, or I'll kill you,' he said, pulling out his revolver.

The two men left the church.

Then, alone, trembling, Giame summoned up his courage and tried to collect his thoughts. An irresistible wave of despair washed over him and he raised the weapon to his temple. But he couldn't, he didn't want to die. He felt defiled, it seemed to him that the world he had up to now thought beautiful was an endless chain of wickedness and vileness.

And this chain began with Ghisparru, the ignorant rustic who through his own foolish soft-heartedness betrayed justice;

and ended with himself, the refined and conscientious man, who did not know how to die, even when confronted by the baseness of his father and the whole world.

But examining himself more closely, he realised that there was a thread of light which still bound him to life. And as his ideas slowly reordered themselves, so this thread thickened, became a glowing beam.

The vast shadow lifted a little.

So then he rose to his feet, approached the altar, picked up an object and went outside. He crossed the silent courtyards and went in search of Ghisparru.

The moon, in its final quarter, had hardly appeared above the black line of the bushes and scrub that closed off the horizon. Its angled gleam threw a strange spell over the heath. The bushes and thickets, illuminated from one side, cast on the dark grass on the other side great creeping shadows. A profound silence, a mysterious peacefulness. The dew was falling and mingling with the scents of night.

The servant had slipped into a doze, but even in this light and troubled sleep he was thinking, in a confused fashion, and waiting.

He heard Giame's steps while they were still some way off and woke up; but he did not move, and he closed his eyes again when the young master came near.

'Ghisparru? Step-father?' Giame called. 'Where are you?'

The servant kept silent, but could feel his heart beat violently. Giame eventually spotted him, came over, dropped to the grass.

'Step-father, wake up, it's me!' he said, shaking him.

The servant pretended to wake, sat up and gazed into

Giame's face.

The moon shone before them picking out the long stalks of hay and flooding the pink bowls of the poppies.

'What do you want?' the old servant asked. 'Why are you so pale?'

Then he regretted the question. He thought: 'That was a mistake! I shouldn't have noticed anything!'

Giame did not know how to begin. His throat felt constricted and he seemed to be acting in a dream.

That low, oblique moon, that great mysterious landscape, that rough and rugged figure crouched beside him in the grass, brought back to him strange shadowy dreams from his adolescence. Distant memories ran through his mind. He remembered an occasion when he had wanted to accompany his father on a stag hunt, in the countryside round Goceano. And to make him stay quiet, while they were waiting in position, crouching low in the grass just like this, Ghisparru had told him a frightening legend. It had been a night just like this.

Then, unexpectedly, there came into his thoughts the tall and innocent figure of the peasant girl who had recited for him a graceful verse in the Logudorese dialect. Then he remembered the whole horrible story recounted by Bellia. He felt again the great shadows swirl round him, catch him by the throat as they had in those first moments of horror. And without even knowing what he was doing, he threw himself flat on the ground, mouth in the grass, chewing at it, sobbing and weeping convulsively.

All this in an instant.

Ghisparru took him by the shoulders, spoke gently to him

and brought him back to his senses.

Then he strongly regretted his tears and related the whole matter to the old man.

The servant listened without batting an eyelid. 'And you believed him?' he asked.

'And do you deny it?' Giame said, angrily. 'Deny it if you can!'

'I deny it. By the milk my wife gave you, my son, what you heard is a complete lie.'

There was a trembling in the rough voice. Giame felt as if a large stone was dissolving inside his chest; but he did not give way quite yet.

'No, it's true, it's true! *Zio* Juanne Battista has confessed.'

'That old goat? That so-called hermit?' Ghisparru exclaimed indignantly. 'What else can he say, a robber of saints? It is true that Antonio Dalvy changed his money for him, but the money was good. The forgeries were Bellia's, and Bellia had those already, he didn't take them from the warden. And the night of the thirteenth of June, he never moved from my side.'

'But how does he know the story of what happened that night, then, with all the details?'

'How should I know?'

'And how does he know, then, that the warden stole the money belonging to the Saint?'

'All kinds of secrets get shared in prison, my son. Some companion will have told him those stories. And then he's gathered all these threads together, the evil crow, and spun this yarn of his to put the wind up Antonio Dalvy. Because if he doesn't get his job back from your father, no one else is going to employ him again.'

Giame drank in the blessed words avidly. It seemed to him the falling dew was sprinkling generous drops of refreshment on his head, easing the painful ring that clamped his forehead. But he remained grave and thoughtful.

At a certain point, while Ghisparru carried on talking, convincing him of Bellia's low cunning, he took out the object he had seized from the altar of Saint John.

It was a small metal chalice, which shone in the moonlight.

'See this, step-father,' he said, showing it to him. 'I took it from the altar of Saint John the Baptist. You believe in God. Well then, this chalice has contained and is still wet with the blood of Our Lord Jesus Christ. So, then, swear on this chalice that on the night of June thirteenth eighteen-ninety-four, Bellia never moved from your side.'

Ghisparru felt himself die; but not even for an instant did he hesitate to accomplish the sacrilege.

He knelt, he crossed himself, he put the palm of his hand on the chalice and he swore.

Only then did Giame feel freed from his oppressive nightmare. But he felt it as if he was emerging from a serious illness, and he let himself fall back on the grass, sinking into it, seeking repose in the dream of the moon, with the infinite sweetness of a convalescent.

* Marquis de Morès. A French-born nobleman and military officer. He spent time in the US and Asia and was famed as a duellist and adventurer.

** Zio Juanne Battista. *Zio*, literally uncle, was the informal title given to middle-aged and elderly men of low social status. Cf the English prefixing of a man's name with 'Old': Old John, etc.

*** A scudo was worth about five lire in Sardinia at this period (1890s).

SARRA

The first week after Easter saw the annual festival of Saint Constantine, in the heights of Bottuda.

The heights of Bottuda are stretches of open country some distance away from the village of the same name, and to get to the little church at the centre of the festivities one has to cross a valley, go through a wood and traverse a broad plain. But the people of Bottuda are very fond of their Saint Constantine, and all winter they dream of making the journey across that valley, through that wood and over that plain, for the sheer pleasure of celebrating the Saint by dancing, singing and drinking: brandy and white wine until mid-day, aniseed liquor and red wine until it is time to return home.

And it is right that they should entertain themselves at last. They have worked all through the harsh winter, ploughing and sowing the rugged ground, watching over their lean and shivering flocks. Now the sheep have grown long coats, the corn is turning green on its stalks, the heathland bushes are in flower and the sky is blue. It is necessary to thank Saint Constantine for the goodly promises of the soil and the flock, and drink and dance and sing in his honour.

Sarra Fioreddu, too, was dreaming of the festival, of the dancing and the travelling hawkers with their colourful rolls of cloth and their fake jewellery. But she did not dare even to speak of her desire.

In her house, they cruelly mistreated her because she refused to marry a sheep-farmer who owned a hundred sheep, horses, land and a dog famous throughout all the neighbouring villages.

'What do I care about his sheep and his dog? I hope it rips its master's throat out!' Sarra would say. 'Mattia looks like a hairy dog himself, with his big nose and his blood-shot eyes. And anyway, he's twenty years older than me, he's short and he's fat. I don't want him, he disgusts me. I'd sooner die.'

She was tall and slender, although she stooped a little, but very beautiful and pale complexioned; in addition to which, she had blue eyes, a rarity in that district. She was lively and fun-loving: she wanted to marry a fresh-faced young man, not a hairy one, someone tall and slim like herself, someone whose embroidered belt could girdle a woman's life.

Her father and her brothers — coarse, hard-drinking men — had absolutely set their minds on her marrying Mattia, the well-to-do sheep-farmer, and mistreated her cruelly.

She could not open her mouth without feeling the threat of being grabbed and dragged about by the hair. Around her she saw nothing but fierce faces, eyes green with anger, and heard nothing but abusive language. She only had to enter the room for her parent and her siblings to take on the aspect of rabid dogs.

But she never gave in. She would say:

'Bully me then, pull my hair out, break me in pieces: the very last piece will say no, no, no.'

In the first few days of April she learnt that her father and brothers, along with their fiancées, were intending to go to the festival of Saint Constantine. They were already making all manner of plans.

'We'll take this, we'll take that; we'll eat under the tree on the right of the church; we'll sing songs about so-and-so; we'll buy this, we'll buy that.'

Sarra listened wide-eyed, flushed with envy; she chafed with rage; she often wept bitterly in the night. Ah, never before had she felt the sting of her misfortunes so deeply. Not to be able to go to the festival while even beggars went; not to be able to express her desire; to be unable even to speak!

All this increased her hatred and repugnance for Mattia. She wept with rage; when she thought of him she clenched her fists, spat, heaped endless insults on him in her own mind. And if she saw him she turned her back and went pale with loathing.

Meanwhile Easter came and went. Preparations for the festival began.

Sweet cakes were made, and bread; the lamb was taken from its pen; oranges were bought, along with red wine, golden Nasco wine, and the first honey was collected. Sarra's heart ached with desire and rancour. She knew that Mattia would not be going to the festival and that increased her own longing.

The night before the festival, the girl slept little and cried copiously. Then she dreamed that she had gone after all and she was dancing with a tall and handsome young man; and when she woke, she felt as if something had tightened around her heart.

She got up while it was still dark. In the kitchen, ranged in a row, were the bags, filled and ready, the bridles laid out, the bits, the spurs, all newly cleaned. In the small yard the horses were nibbling at the scattered straw; and in the silence of the mild air there came from time to time the metallic sound of their hooves on the dew-damp cobbles.

Sarra looked, listened, lit the fire, put the coffee on to boil and began to cry again.

Her father, who was sleeping on a mat, woke and yawned. Then he asked in a curt and sleepy voice: 'What's the matter with you? What are you crying for?'

Sarra felt her heart soften a little, almost touched, but at the same time she was afraid. She broke into loud sobs but made no answer.

Her father got up. He bent over a bag and lifted it as if to test its weight.

'Pity the devil hasn't stolen your shoes,' he said to Sarra, still holding the bag. 'Did you want to come to Saint Constantine's festival?'

She continued to sob, face hidden in her apron. Her father pulled it aside menacingly:

'Answer your father. Do you or don't you want to come to the festival?'

'Yes,' she replied in a voice as thin as thread.

'Yes!' her father said, mimicking her. 'Well, the devil can

take you there. Go, go and change your shawl and shoes.'

Sarra hurried away.

Then the brothers got up as well, rolled up their mats, stood them on end along the walls, and exchanged glances. 'She's coming,' they said in lowered voices.

'Ah,' the father was saying to himself, while picking out his horse's bridle, 'there shouldn't have been any need for this.'

Sarra reappeared very soon, pink, rather breathless, with her eyes still swollen but now shining with joy. She had changed in a matter of minutes; she had put on a snow-white shift, her new shoes, a waistcoat trimmed with gold lace, and over her hair a large, fringed headscarf in violet damask. When their mounts were ready she sat up behind her father on his grey mare. And off they went, across the valley, through the wood and over the plain, in the pure and fragrant April morning.

During the journey, not one of Sarra's relations, not even her future sisters-in-law, addressed a word to her; but she did not mind. She laughed and chattered with the other local people going to the festival, and was happy beyond expression.

The dew shone on the heads of corn; birds sang in the bushes; the air was saturated with perfumes. The most handsome youths in Bottuda were making their way to the festival. They turned their heads to look at Sarra, whose face, beneath the headscarf of violet damask, looked like a heathland rose. She laughed and spoke loudly so that the youths would hear her, her blue gaze turned on them with seeming ingenuousness, full of life and joy.

'We shall dance together,' said the eyes of the young men

and Sarra's. 'And what a time we shall have.'

And indeed she thoroughly enjoyed herself all day long: she found her girlfriends, she danced, she flirted, she was courted by all the young men.

Her father and her brothers drank brandy and white wine, aniseed and red wine, played at cards and target-shooting and paid her no attention at all.

She did everything she had wanted to do, anything that took her fancy and never gave a thought to Mattia or to the persecution she had suffered. She bought rings with yellow and green stones, received a number of gallant tokens from admirers and hid everything in her bosom.

By the time the hour for departure drew near, she was tired of dancing, her feet were on fire, her jaws ached from laughing and the violet headscarf was falling over her burning face, but it was still with sorrow that she saw the moment when they must leave approaching.

The sun was sinking, the sky was lighting up with gold on the horizon, the little church was stretching a long shadow over the trampled grass; a great silence was already descending over the plain. The dream was at an end.

A few at a time, people gradually began to drift off: almost all the men were drunk, the women melancholy. The Fioreddus were among the last to leave, and the father lingered longer than anyone else. He was drunk too, but pretending to be so more than he really was. He staggered, he closed his eyes, he muddled his words. Once on his horse he swayed this way and that in the saddle, and Sarra almost had to hold him up to prevent him from falling. The mare walked slowly, allowing itself to be caught up and overtaken by the hawkers' carts and even by the beggars making their way back on foot. In a slow stream they passed, until old Fioreddu and his daughter were all by themselves, the very last ones, on the path that led into the wood. The shadows were falling: through the motionless branches, in the quiet of dusk, the colour was draining from a pallid sky. The revolving of cartwheels, the treading of horses' hooves, the voices and the singing faded in the distance.

Old Fioreddu still swayed in the saddle and appeared to have gone to sleep. A heavy sadness descended on Sarra. Her face was very pale, her eyes, so ready for laughter or tears, clouded over.

It frightened her to be alone in the wood like this with that drunken man, and she did not dare wake him and tell him to ride faster.

She tried her best to dig her heels into the mare's sides, but the animal shook its tail, pricked up its ears and carried on walking at the same slow pace. It was full of food, sated on grass and leaves and had no interest, as when old Fioreddu was returning from a day's work, in trotting eagerly towards its manger.

Sarra began to be both angry and worried. Darkness was falling, the sounds of the carts and the voices of the people making their way home had vanished. Old Fioreddu continued to sleep.

'Constantine, my Saint,' Sarra said to herself, 'what is happening? Help us, or it'll be tomorrow morning by the time we get home.'

All at once she had a tremendous fright: she thought she saw Mattia behind a tree, in the last glimmerings of dusk.

'It's the devil,' she thought, but immediately gave a

piercing cry and clung to her father's waist, because Mattia really did appear, leaping out in front of them and stopping the horse.

He was carrying a rifle, a pistol and a knife and looked like a highwayman. Two other men came running behind him, whom Sarra knew well. They were two of Mattia's servants.

The girl instantly realised they meant to abduct her, and began to yell, clutching her father and calling for help. Fioreddu seemed to wake up.

'What's the matter?' he asked, in a hoarse and sleepy voice. 'What do you want, Mattia?'

'Get down off the horse,' the other replied. 'Leave me your daughter and the mare and go home on foot, back to the village. I'll bring both of them back to you in good condition.'

Old Fioreddu started to laugh and said:

'Ha! You're joking! Are you wanting to go to the festival, now, at this hour? You must be mad. We're just on our way home from the festival now.'

'Yes, it's easy to see!' Mattia said. 'How many bottles have you drunk? Enough, get down nicely or I'll make you get down the hard way.'

'No! No!' Sarra shouted. 'Don't leave me, my papa. I'll do everything you want, but don't leave me here now.'

It was useless. Her cries echoed through the wood in vain; half dead, she found herself, after lashing out briefly with fists, nails and kicks, at her captor's mercy.

Old Fioreddu, who was laughing and babbling nonsensically, was left in the wood, and Sarra was led to the captor's den.

There, in his house, was Mattia's sister, an ugly, swarthy

woman with thick lips, who tried to comfort the girl.

'Don't be scared, my dove,' she told her, 'no one's going to harm a hair on your head. Tomorrow morning, Mattia, he'll take you back home, and the mare too, he'll take her with him. And the two of you will be married straightaway, my dove, don't be scared.'

'No, I don't believe you, horse-lips,' said Sarra defiantly. 'You may be a bunch of wild animals, but I won't marry your brother.'

'What do you mean, sister dear?' said the other woman, spreading a sleeping mat beside the fire. 'Who do you think will marry you now? After this business, who do you expect to marry you? Lie down, keep calm, once you're with my brother you'll be like a queen. Lie down, my Sarrina. Tomorrow morning we'll make coffee, and afterwards we'll all go back to the village, and tomorrow morning Mattia himself will give you his wedding gift: eight rings with precious stones, a silver medallion, embroidered shoes, a headscarf the colour of carnations.'

The woman continued to list the presents the husband would give, but Sarra turned her back and crouched in a corner of the room.

Ah, she saw it all clearly. It had been a hideous piece of play-acting, and they had all connived in it together, including her brothers and her father. What could she do, against those wild animals, as she called them?

'What shall I do?' she thought, sobbing. 'Shall I go to the magistrates and denounce these wild animals? And then? They'll convict them, but no one will want to marry me any more after I've been carried off like this. They'll all believe

I've spent the night with that dog Mattia, and no one will look at me again.'

She wept for a long time with these thoughts swirling in her head; she lapsed into blank despair; little by little she calmed down, and towards dawn she began to doze. And then, into her heart, in her half-waking state, stole an idea of strange and savage sweetness.

'Those wild beasts!' she thought hazily. 'They have overpowered me. But then it will be my turn. Ah, dear brothers, you think you're going to profit from Mattia's wealth? But I shall be the mistress, I'll drive you away like scabby dogs. And you, Mattia, you think you'll have a faithful wife? I will marry you, but you're making a mistake, you wild beast…'

And with that thought, she went to sleep.

THE FIRST KISSES

Standing on a grassy mound overlooking the country road, Jorgj Preda, nicknamed Tiligherta, had been waiting for more than a quarter of an hour. He was expecting his little sweetheart, Nania, the road-keeper's daughter.

They had been tentatively in love now for three weeks; that is, since they first came to know each other. Nania took this country road every day to fetch water from the stream and carry it back to the road-keeper's cottage. And Jorgj waited for her on the grassy mound, pretending to be minding the sheep, which at this time of day were deep in their afternoon slumbers among the bushes beneath the shady canopy of the cork-oak forest.

The moment the figure of Nania appeared on the white and deserted road, Jorgj would scramble down from his look-out point and wait in the shade, behind the knoll, where Nania joined him, full of love and fear, and still carrying on her head the tall, decorated pitcher which resembled an Etruscan amphora.

For it was certain that if her papa had found her sweet-talking with Jorgj he would have beaten her until her ribs cracked. At this hour of the day old Gavinu Faldedda would be taking his customary nap or working on the small-holding attached to the road-keeper's cottage, but even so they had to be careful.

The two young people would chatter away to each other for five or six minutes, devouring each other with their eyes but not exchanging so much as a touch of the finger-tips. Then Nania went sedately on her way and Jorgj would plunge into the forest with pained sighs.

He felt proud and happy, certainly, to possess a sweetheart all of his own, out here, in total solitude, far away from where anyone lived; but his happiness was anything but complete.

First of all there was that pest, old Gavinu — who would never think of marrying Nania off to a ragamuffin like Jorgj — and then… a whole pile of thens… well, anyway. Suffice it to say, Jorgj, in the face of conscription and many other calamities to come, would have been content to receive at least a kiss from Nania. But this was the worst part, the thing that really made him sigh: the girl had not the slightest intention of kissing him and he, on his account, did not dare touch even the hem of her skirt. On that particular day, however, Jorgj had resolved to enfold her in his arms and say to her: 'But if people who love each other don't exchange a kiss, who do you suppose does?'

But just on this very day Nania failed to appear.

Still standing on the mound, Jorgj began to grow anxious, because he could tell from the long shadow thrown by the staff he clutched that it was well past two.

Jorgj Preda, who was known locally as Tiligherta, came from the village of Bitti and was about nineteen years old.

Along with an old shepherd from Nuoro, he tended the flocks of a well-to-do man also from Nuoro, and the pastures where they grazed stretched as far as one of the road-keeper's sections on the Bitti road.

Jorgj could have claimed to be a handsome youth — he believed himself to be a mature man — tall and muscular, though slender, with the blackest of black hair and a perfect profile; one of those sculpted profiles, of the best Greek school, that are seen only in the Bitti and Orune district. But his skin had been too darkened and hardened by sun and cold weather, and the soft line of his pretty mouth, his fine lips and his gleaming teeth could not relieve the harsh gaze of his clouded and almost sombre black eyes.

Brought up in Nuoro, Jorgj spoke the Nuorese dialect with a faint overlay of his native pronunciation. But he retained the costume of his own village, almost entirely black apart from the tight white britches, somewhat torn and dirty.

Since he had discovered the road-keeper's cottage and had fallen in love with the little daughter of old Gavinu, Jorgj Tiligherta had been washing his face and hands and trying to clean himself up, but despite his efforts he remained as black as the devil, and his heavy boots and his cap still gave off the less than voluptuous perfume of the sheep pen.

And still Nania did not appear. A hundred ugly thoughts crowded the young shepherd's restless mind, making him sadder with every minute that the shadow of his staff lengthened on the fresh new grass of the knoll.

His eyes half closed, Jorgj remained rigid on its summit, fiercely scrutinising the furthest point of the road, and not a human soul passed across the immense space of the surrounding countryside.

In the soft April afternoon, the oak woods which covered the untamed highlands, all entangled with cistus, arbutus and brambles, stood peaceful and silent. Their fresh foliage seemed to contain the reflection of a pearly blue sky. They stretched as far as the eye could see, right to the vanishing horizon and the deeper and more vaporous blue of the distant mountains that closed it off. From where Jorgj was standing, the roof of the road-keeper's cottage only just rose into view. A long, diaphanous spiral of smoke could be seen curling from its chimney, but the shepherds' hut was out of sight, much further off in the dense interior of the forest.

The road snaked across the landscape, between the woods, like a river-bed parched dry by the sun, and grass grew along its sides, still tall and beautiful because the sheep had so much rich pasturage up here on the heath that they had not needed to go near it.

Nania was not coming, Nania would not appear now. Jorgj's eyes, which a little while before had been glowing with unusual brightness at the thought of the kisses he would bestow, wanted or not, on his young sweetheart, grew ever darker and became almost obscured by tears. Ah, Saint George, my saint, something must have happened. Perhaps Nania was ill. Perhaps old Gavinu had sensed something and was refusing to let her fetch the water any more. Perhaps… Jorgj was getting ready to leave his sentry post and make his way to the cottage on some pretext or other, as he often did, when he heard the galloping of two horses and saw, through a light cloud of dust, two fine-looking gentlemen ride past without so much as glancing at him.

He paid little attention to them either, since he often saw people coming along the road. He scrambled down from the mound and set off. But half way there he stopped in surprise. The sight of the tall, decorated pitcher which he knew so well caused his heart to beat. But not for long. It was not Nania carrying it on her head, not Nania advancing along the barren whiteness of the country lane, with the yellow headscarf trailing over her shoulders and making a bright flare in the sunshine. It was her little sister, Arrosa.

'Why is it you going for the water today?' he called out, sounding angry.

Instead of answering, Arrosa, a little rascal of the worst sort, broke into a sing-song chant as soon as she recognised who it was, just to annoy him:

'Tiligherta, tiligherta,

'Your mama is such a flirter,

'Your papa is close to dying,

'Tiligherta, always lying…'

But he took no notice and repeated the question, less harshly, as he came up to the little girl.

Arrosa, fearing a smack, then gave him a pretty smile and replied:

'Because Nania is busy working.'

'And what kind of busy work is that?'

'She's busy working because the road-manager and the

engineer are coming. Didn't you see them go by?'

'Ah, that was those two men? Do they come very often?'

'Well now! Sometimes they come often and sometimes not very often. What does it matter to you?'

Jorgj considered whether he should accompany the girl to the stream to find out more about these men. Already he was cross with them and felt a stirring of jealousy, since it was because of them that he had missed seeing Nania this afternoon. As they came towards the grassy knoll he pointed to where the sheep lay and said:

'Would you like a little lamb, a little lamb as white as a dog's teeth?'

Arrosa thought he was teasing her, and in revenge repeated the nonsense rhyme, chanting it in a mixture of dialects, Nuoro, Campidano and Ozieri. But Jorgj repeated the offer with such sincerity that he succeeded in obtaining plenty of details about the two men.

The manager was from Nuoro and the engineer, the one with the blond beard, from the mainland.

And this engineer was a person Arrosa had known for a long, long time. Every time he came to the road-keeper's cottage he gave Nania a handsome tip, part of which she gave to her papa and part she hid in a little bag under her mattress. And to her, to Arrosa, he never gave anything, ever... That was why she couldn't bear the sight of him.

'What's his name?' Jorgj asked, pulling a wry face.

'Signor Gugliemo.'

'Do they stay the night?'

'Yes.'

All at once Jorgj turned his back on the girl and walked

off, hollow-faced.

'Tiligherta,' Arrosa shouted after him, 'don't forget the lamb, the little lamb…'

He made no reply and very soon disappeared into the depths of the woods. He was tormented by a dreadful jealousy. He returned to the hut, but in such a bad mood that he quarrelled with old Concafrisca, the other shepherd, and they very nearly came to blows. He went out again to tramp the woods, trailing his misery through the sweet-smelling clumps of cistus, in the gentle, rosy sunset, and was unable to do a thing all that evening.

As night began to descend he made his way to the road-keeper's cottage but did not have the courage to enter. For a long time he prowled round outside, like a damned soul, but only when it was dark did he draw near.

Although a thin strand of smoke still rose from the chimney to lose itself in the misty air of the cool April night, the door was shut fast, the windows closed and a heavy silence surrounded the house. From the window of the engineer's room, on the ground floor, the glow from a lamp cast a square of light on the road.

Jorgj Preda crept close and saw, through the panes of glass, the man with the blond beard, the one Arrosa had said was the engineer, in his shirtsleeves.

No doubt he was preparing for bed. He was tall and thin, fair-haired and had small eyes whose colour was indiscernible but which narrowed at the corners in a curious fashion, giving his whole face an agreeable expression. A good-looking man, in short, who might have been of any age, it was impossible to tell.

Jorgj was staring at him intently when he saw Nania enter the room. He trembled all over and made an involuntary leap, twisting backwards and sideways, to prevent the girl from seeing him.

Nania was a small girl, slender and unsmiling. In her fifteen-year-old's very serious face there constantly fluttered a trace of sadness, and the dull pallor of her fine-skinned complexion was accentuated by the ashy tint of her blonde hair. The splendour of her luxuriant curls, which must have weighed heavy on her small lilywhite head, told of a child grown up before her time. And indeed, for three or four years, since the death of her mother, she had kept house at the road-keeper's cottage.

She did everything, with scarcely any help from Arrosa, and did not waste a minute of the day. Except that for three weeks she had appeared distracted, neglecting her domestic tasks and spending an unusual amount of time going to fetch the water. At certain moments she was overcome by outbreaks of wild gaiety, and at others she shed floods of tears. Old Gavinu observed the change, but said nothing and was unable to guess the cause.

From the road, Jorgj, miserable and on edge, gazed with shining eyes through the window. He was quite overcome by a sweet sense of tenderness and passion at seeing this small and fragile young woman again, who had bewitched him and for whom he would have turned his shotgun on the king himself.

Nania was wearing the costume of the Ozieri district, where old Gavinu Faldedda came from, but with the headscarf on her shoulders in the Campidano manner. Her corseted waistcoat of faded brocade was tightened at the front with multi-stringed red laces and buttoned at the wrists over a sleeveless chemise.

The skirt and apron were of dark cotton in the plainest style, and Nania wore no ornament but a small coral necklace round her slim and vulnerable throat. She was bare-headed and bare-footed as she came into the engineer's room, carrying a jug of water.

Jorgj saw his sweetheart smile at the handsome gentleman, and the latter send her in return a look and a smile filled with love. Nimble and gracious, Nania set the jug down in a corner, then moved to stand near the engineer. They spoke. From his position outside, Jorgj could hear nothing, but was shaken by giddy surges of rage and jealousy. Ah, there was no doubting it, there was no doubting it… Nania was deceiving him, what Nania liked were gentleman who were not only rich and handsome but clean.

The blood rushed to Jorgj's face and his temples throbbed. If he had had a shotgun he would have discharged it straight through the window glass, killing that fine gentleman who was robbing him of his very life.

All at once he turned pale and leapt back again, even more dismayed and agitated than before.

Ah, what was this he was seeing now…? He thought he would go mad, and he never forgot the sensation he felt at that moment.

After much talking and smiling, the engineer had taken Nania's little head between his two hands, his two long-fingered hands, with a touch as light and delicate as a woman's, and had covered her face with kisses. Then he had drawn her into his arms, holding her to his chest in a long embrace, while the girl smiled and wept all at the same time. Out in the road, Jorgj groaned. The engineer must have heard something, for he suddenly let Nania go and strode to the window. Jorgj had the presence of mind to step back and press himself to the wall and was not seen. He saw the square of light, however, disappear from the road's surface and realised that the shutters had been closed.

He was seized by a great spasm of rage, and a somewhat base and cowardly idea: to hammer on the road-keeper's door and tell old Gavinu:

'Just you see what's happening in your own house, just you see…!' But he did not do that. He decided instead to murder the engineer; and this idea had an almost calming effect. He walked away, while strange, dry sobs racked and twisted his throat…

At dawn, Jorgj Preda, concealed behind a thicket of brambles a quarter of an hour's walk from the cottage, armed with old Concafrisca's shotgun, was waiting for the engineer to pass to blast him to kingdom come. The previous afternoon, Arrosa had told him that the two men would be travelling on the next day to visit the other road-keeper in the district, and they must therefore pass this way. And so he was waiting… with a fierce resolve etched on his painfully troubled face, and his eyes more sombre and clouded than usual. In the cool April dawn the countryside was enchanting under a magical haze of glimmering light and fragile scents. To the east a smoky gold coloured the wooded horizon. And in the dew-tipped bushes the birds were happily singing. But Jorgj Preda's attention was focussed on anything but the idyllic poetry of a spring morning.

From his hiding place behind the brambles he could look down on a long stretch of road and see the bridge beneath which ran a slack ribbon of water, flanked by tall reeds and asphodels just coming into flower.

And he thought back to the dreams he had often dreamed, sitting on the parapet of the bridge, to the songs he had sung at the top of his voice — accompanied by the rustling of the oaks and the clinking of the sheep's bells — in the hope they might be heard by Nania far away. This was where the flock came to drink every night, rather than at the other stream which Jorgj treated as a sacred river since its water served the road-keeper's house.

From time to time, the young shepherd's mind was swayed by these tender memories and he thought he should just go away, wondering if it had not all been a bad dream, but the reality of the situation soon gripped him again and he did not move.

But the men he was waiting for did not appear and every passing minute seemed like a century, all the more since other people might come along and discover him there; and in his state of anxiety he feared missing his shot as well.

Here they came at last! The sun was about to rise over the glowing horizon of the forest when Jorgj spotted their horses and heard the hated voice of his rival. He edged his way through the tangled thickets of his hiding place, peering, hawk-like, with hungry eyes. They fixed on the engineer, studying him more closely than he had been able to do the previous night. His finely-shaped lips, turned white and pinched by the desperation of that long and hellish night, compressed into a bitter smile.

Ah, look at that man, a gentleman, handsome, well-mannered. What did he, Jorgj Preda — Tiligherta — count for with his black face and his ragged clothes, what did he count for in comparison with that clear-skinned, fair-haired gentleman, so well-dressed and elegant? Nania, slender and graceful like a lady, was quite right to prefer him. But then why, if she liked gentlemen, why had she cast her spell on him, telling him he was the one she wanted and that she would wait until they could be married?

On the point of killing a man, Jorgj Preda felt a sudden desire to weep. The men were coming closer. In his mind's eye Jorgj saw Nania once more, his little Nania whom he still adored as he adored Our Lady of the Miracle, in the embrace of the engineer; and he raised old Concafrisca's ancient shotgun.

As he moved into his field of fire, the engineer, not thinking of the terrible danger that lurked just above him, lifted his head, removed his white country cap, briefly balancing it on the saddle bow, and a moment later smiled, still arguing things over with his companion, with his face turned towards Jorgj's bramble bush. He seemed to be looking straight at him. The sun broke over the treetops and the rosy yellow of its first beams flooded across the road and fell on the figures of the two riders.

Jorgj did not fire and let his rival pass unharmed.

He had seen the engineer's eyes and his smile, and a strange thought, unexpectedly flashing into his disturbed mind, had stayed his hand.

At two o'clock, leaning on the long staff — his shepherd's crook — as upright and rigid on the grassy, daisy-covered mound as on that earlier day, Jorgj was looking out for Nania's approach. He had taken himself off in the morning to Nuoro market with his calling card, that is, with the fresh cheese, ricotta and milk, and had then changed into new clothes entirely and now, in the solid whiteness of his shirt and with his face blanched by the terrible emotion he had suffered, he looked a different, almost lighter man. The suffering and lack of sleep had narrowed his features, so much so that Nania, as soon as they were in the shadows of the mound, said:

'Why are you looking so handsome today…?'

The young girl's voice had a gentle and sad tone, rendered more affecting by the distinct Logudoro accent.

At first Jorgj, a sombre expression in his eyes, did not answer and just gazed at her intently as if trying to see inside her soul.

'You're much more beautiful…' he replied, sounding cross. And clumsily taking the pitcher from her he set it on the ground and said:

'We need to have a long talk today, Nanì…'

She was scared and looked at him in alarm. With her wide headscarf, flowered on a golden yellow background, spreading across her shoulders like a shawl, Jorgj found her so beautiful that he suddenly softened and remained gazing at her in ecstasy. She resembled one of those holy figures depicted in Spanish tapestries or admired in Italian paintings of the sixteenth century, and Jorgj, thinking of the darker beauties of the girls he had known up to then, grew all the more certain in his doubts.

'Sit down,' he said, making her sit on a nearby stone, 'so that we can talk.'

'I can't stop, I can't stop...' she said, trembling. 'My father...'

'Your father is a long way away and no one will see us. And even if anyone did see us, what harm is there in that...? Can't we be friends, acquaintances...?'

'My God, my God, I can't...'

In truth, the idea of sitting for a while at Jorgj's side gave Nania intense pleasure, and although she still felt scared she did not move.

'What's wrong with you today?' she asked him, trembling. 'What's the matter? Are you cross because I didn't come yesterday, perhaps? You know the manager and the engineer were here and I had a lot of work to do. There's no one else to run the house.'

She fell silent, her eyes lost in sad and painful thoughts. Jorgj, seeing her turn paler than ever, no doubt remembering the engineer, twitched with rage and edged away from her side.

He continued to study the girl's face and a great darkness settled over his spirits. No, there was no doubt. Nania was deceiving him and the engineer was her lover.

'What's wrong with you, what's the matter?' she repeated.

'What's the matter?' Jorgj shouted, waving his arms like a madman. 'You know better than I do what's the matter...'

'I don't know anything! Are you losing your mind?'

'Yes, I think I must be losing my mind. Nania, listen, you're only little but you're much more spiteful than me. All the same, you're not going to go on laughing at me, no, you won't go on. You took me for a nice young man but I'm not, no. I'm just a poor wretch, but you shouldn't have laughed at me because I can make you pay dearly for that sort of game,

Nanì, do you hear, Nanì?'

Nania looked at him in stupefaction and could find nothing to say in the face of his fury.

'Answer me!' Jorgj shouted.

'Don't make so much noise…' the girl said, jumping up and turning her head to listen. 'If my father hears us…'

'What do I care if he does? Since I've got nothing to do with you any more…'

'But what's wrong with you, what have they been telling you?' she asked in desperation.

'Nothing, no one's been telling me anything. I've seen for myself, with my own eyes. I saw last night. Yes, why did the two of you leave the shutters open, my beauty? And this morning I had him there, in my sights, right between the eyes. I was ready to murder your handsome gentleman. I didn't do it because I had a sudden mad idea. I saw him smile and it seemed to me he resembled you and I thought, see how mad this is, I thought: who knows, he could be her father… Now I realise it was a crazy thing to think. Your father! Your father is old Gavinu, devil take him, and you are… you are…' Jorgj concluded, spilling out a terrible accusation, 'you are the engineer's mistress.'

All the colours of the rainbow rushed over Nania's grieving countenance. Her heart, her little impassioned heart, seemed to want to burst through the faded brocade of the old jacket and big tears quivered brilliantly in her eyes. She made no attempt at denial, and did not even speak. Filled with a great, childlike fear, imagining Jorgj might be about to harm her, her one thought was to escape and she moved so suddenly and swiftly that the young man had difficulty catching her up, in the roadway.

'Nania,' he exclaimed, smiling against his will and gripping her arm, 'I didn't believe you could be so bad… Why are you running away? Were you frightened I was going to kill you perhaps…?'

Even she could not help smiling. The scarf had slipped from her head altogether and that little head of golden hair was flooded with the full light of the sun.

Jorgj let out an exclamation of joy and amazement on seeing her smiling face and her blue eyes — a green-tinted blue — exactly like the engineer's.

'Nania, Nania, forgive me,' he said, smiling and beginning to cry at the same time. 'Come here, come here and let's make our peace. As God's my witness, and Our Lady of the Miracle too, I won't say a word of this to anyone. I won't even speak of it to you, no never, never, never again. Come over here and collect your pitcher, come on, come on.'

Virtually taking her in his arms he led her back into the shade behind the grassy mound. Nania might have been without life, so pale and still were her features. But when Jorgj said:

'Who could have believed it, who could have thought it… your mother…' Nania drew herself erect, her face flushed, her eyes blazing with anger yet full of tears and shouted:

'My mother is dead! Respect her, because she was a saint. The engineer kissed me and embraced me because I am the one he loves… Kill me then, Jorgj Preda, kill me, but don't bring my mother into it…'

She collapsed on the ground and burst into tears. With those words she was losing everything. She was losing the love of Jorgj, whom she adored with all the enthusiasm of her fifteen years, of her first love, she was losing her dreams and her sweetest hopes, she was losing her honour and perhaps putting in danger her own life and that of the engineer. But what did it matter? The memory of her mother — whose guilty secret was known to nobody and especially not to Gavinu Faldedda, who still wept for her, treasuring her memory — would be saved by her sacrifice…

But Jorgj Preda had seen.

For a few moments he stood silent and motionless, looking down at the young girl who sat on the grass, still crying. Her child's despairing sobs were lost in the great silence of the afternoon, and in all the vastness of the sleeping landscape Jorgj could hear no other sound.

And he was all for running away, feeling himself to be base and unworthy beside little Nania, but naturally he could not move a muscle. He remembered instead all the beautiful promises they had exchanged, he remembered the dreams of love, especially those he had dreamed at night while the sheep drank beneath the bridge, down amongst the asphodels and the oleanders; he thought that in less than three years he would be in a position to marry Nania; and he bent down.

'Leave me be…' she said.

But Jorgj lifted her like a feather, took her in his arms and covered her face with kisses until he had succeeded in reassuring her and making her smile.

DEDALUS CELEBRATING WOMEN'S LITERATURE 2018 TO 2028

Dedalus began celebrating the centenary in 2018 of women getting the vote in the UK by a programme of women's fiction. In 1918, Parliament passed an act granting the vote to women over the age of thirty who were householders, the wives of householders, occupiers of property with an annual rent of £5, and graduates of British universities. About 8.4 million women gained the vote. It was a big step forward but It was not until the Equal Franchise Act of 1928 that women over twenty-one were able to vote and women finally achieved the same voting rights as men. This act increased the number of women eligible to vote to fifteen million. Dedalus' aim is to publish six titles each year, most of which will be translations from other European languages, for the next ten years as we commemorate this important milestone.

Titles published so far are:

The Prepper Room by Karen Duve
Take Six: Six Portuguese Women Writers edited by Margaret Jull Costa
Slav Sisters: The Dedalus Book of Russian Women's Literature edited by Natasha Perova
Baltic Belles: The Dedalus Book of Estonian Women's Literature edited by Elle-Mari Talivee
The Madwoman of Serrano by Dina Salústio
Primordial Soup by Christine Leunens

Cleopatra Goes to Prison by Claudia Durastanti
The Girl from the Sea and other stories by Sophia de Mello Breyner Andresen
The Price of Dreams by Margherita Giacobino
The Medusa Child by Sylvie Germain
Days of Anger by Sylvie Germain
Venice Noir by Isabella Panfido
Chasing the Dream by Liane de Pougy
A Woman's Affair by Liane de Pougy
La Madre (The Woman and the Priest) by Grazia Deledda
Fair Trade Heroin by Rachael McGill
Co-wives, Co-widows byAdrienne Yabouza
Catalogue of a Private Life by Najwa Bin Shatwan
Baltic Belles: The Dedalus Book of Latvian Women's Literature edited by Eva Eglaja
This was the Man (Lui) by Louise Colet
This Woman, This Man (Elle et Lui) by George Sand
The Queen of Darkness (and other stories) by Grazia Deledda
The Christmas Present (and other stories) by Grazia Deledda
Cry Baby by Ros Franey
The Scaler of the Peaks by Karin Erlandsson

Forthcoming titles will include:

Take Six: Six Balkan Women Writers edited by Will Firth
Take Six: Six Catalan Women Writers edited by Peter Bush
Take Six: Six Latvian Women Writers edited by Jayde Will
The Queen of Darkness (and other stories) by Grazia Deledda
The Christmas Present (and other stories) by Grazia Deledda
Marianna Sirca by Grazia Deledda

The Dedalus Book of Knitting: Blue Yarn by Karin Erlandsson
The Victor by Karin Erlandsson
My Father's House by Karmele Jaio
Eddo's Souls by Stella Gaitano

For more information contact Dedalus at info@dedalusbooks.
com

La Madre (The Woman and the Priest)
by Grazia Deledda

'The syntax of *La Madre* is uncomplicated, but its descriptions are vivid and moving. As with the reeds and the wind, Deledda draws on elements from everyday surroundings to conjure exquisitely lyrical metaphors: "little by little desire crept into that love of theirs, chaste and pure as a pool of still water beneath a wall that suddenly crumbles and falls in ruin". The theme of the priest's forbidden love is rendered more complex by the towering figure of the mother, and the acute psychological strain provoked in each of the protagonists is superbly portrayed by means of analepses, reminiscences, inner questioning and dreams. This allows for the motives to be viewed from each character's perspective, shifting the reader's sympathy in the course of the novel. It can also lead to opposing evaluation on the reader's part. For the author of *Sons and Lovers*, for example, the mother "succeeds, by her old barbaric maternal power over her son, in finally killing his sex life too". For Steegman, "while she is inexorable with the priest her heart yearns over the young man, tender with his grief", and thus "claims the reader's whole sympathy".'

Vilma de Gasperin in *The Times Literary Supplement*

£8.99   ISBN 978 1 912868 63 6   138p   B. Format

**The Christmas Present (and other stories)
by Grazia Deledda**

A native of Sardinia, Grazia Deledda's novels are mostly
set in the rugged hills around her home town of Nuoro. Her
characters reflect the difficult lives of people still constrained
by ancient customs and practices. Her voice is powerful, her
tone often sombre. But her wide-ranging talent had a sunnier
side, revealed in many of her later works.

The Christmas Present, first published in 1930, brings together
a collection of folk tales, children's stories and personal
reminiscences that portray with humour and affection the
lighter side of Sardinian life. This is a book that will charm
and delight, opening a window on to the Sardinia of old and
the formative influences on one of Italy's most important
twentieth century authors.

£8.99   ISBN   978 1 915568 16 8   142p   B. Format